Born in Germany, Ute Maria lived in Eastern Canada, the USA and then Western Canada, where she met her British husband. In 1978, they moved outside Cambridge, where she taught languages at a private school before becoming Head of Department. She also organised student trips to Russia, Egypt, Turkey, Germany, New York, Washington D.C. and Kenya and travelled all over the world in the holidays.

Ute Maria has written short stories, novels, plays and also for children. Now she volunteers for her local primary school where Max continues his journeys to Jupiter and Saturn.

Max and Milky Make it to Mars

# Ute Maria Sproulle

Max and Milky Make it to Mars

Nightingale Books

A CIP catalogue record for this title is
available from the British Library.

ISBN 9781912021635

*Nightingale Books is an imprint of*
*Pegasus Elliot MacKenzie Publishers Ltd.*
www.pegasuspublishers.com
First Published in 2017

**Nightingale Books**
**Sheraton House Castle Park**
**Cambridge England**
Printed & Bound in Great Britain

# Dedication

To my mother, who was full of love.

# Acknowledgements

To Richard for his continuing support and to Book Club at Petersfield Primary School for their encouragement.

# Introduction

I had never been to Mars before I was 10. Nobody I knew had. Except in their imagination. Mainly my great uncle's imagination. He's Professor Boggle, my mum's uncle. A bit weird, the mad scientist type.

But he got me there - to Mars, and before that to the Moon where I met - okay I'll say it: Martians. I know you won't believe me, sometimes I don't believe it myself so I'll move on.

Milky came too, but more of her later. Her aunt Anna tried to stop us. She's a scientist, like Professor Boggle. But not a good one. In fact, I'd say downright evil. Maybe I had better start at the beginning.

You know how it is when things are getting you down at school and your parents are getting at you about homework and science projects and then they expect you to tidy your room. You really wish you could escape, go somewhere where no one would find you. To the ends of the universe, stuff like that. Well, in my case I was desperate to go to Mars, now that I'd been to the Moon. And I knew just the person to get me there; Professor Septimus Boggle. He was a professor of Physics at the University. Or had been. I never really found out why he had to leave. Until it was too late.

But I'd better tell you about Max - that's me - and how it all happened. And why they locked me up.

# I
# In the Beginning

I liked going to the Professor's house. It was far more interesting than ours which was new and what Dad called 'the best suburbia has to offer.' Big deal. The Professor's was old, two stories and a porch, with lots of trees and long grass to hide in. He never cleaned much, which was fine by me. Mum was always cleaning which meant I had to, too.

My parents didn't mind me going round there. Mum liked her Uncle Septimus but didn't visit much, what with her interior decorating business. She usually spent more time in other people's houses than our own. I'd get home and microwave myself some dinner, or finish off some cake and watch TV - eating was something I did like to do.

Dad often had to go away on business and when he was home he was working. So I'd only see him when he thought I needed to be 'punished'. I'd go to the Professor's after school or on weekends, with a cake. I called him 'Professor' because, well, that's what he was.

And his place was definitely more interesting than school. The teachers preached at you or ignored you and the bullies were lurking round every corner - nobody enjoyed lurking more than Murky. I hated school. You would too if you had to be on the lookout for Murky all the time. He was big, with arms down to here. And he was mean.

Every morning I had to give him my lunch money. If I didn't, he would beat me up. Sometimes he'd beat me up anyway. His favourite trick was catching me in the toilet. Then he'd put my head in the bowl and flush. He called it 'doing a swirly' - his speciality. I was getting pretty good at holding my breath under water. Those toilets seemed to flush forever.

One day he steals my homework. He promises he won't beat me up if I don't tell. So Mr Hickey, the science teacher, asks me for my homework. I tell him I forgot it. I get detention. Murky gets an 'A'. And I still get beat up! To top it off, my dad punishes me as well. I was grounded for a week, no going to Uncle Septimus's house.

So I snuck out. Nobody was going to keep me from going to the Professor's. He just made everything sound so interesting - including science (which was more than boring old Hickey-Stickey ever could).

The Professor would show me his drawings and plans for his latest inventions. And he would even discuss them with me - as if I were a grown-up, as if I had ideas of my own!

But the best thing was his workshop, out in the garage or should I say barn. Full of machines and test tubes and hissing vats and weird stuff. I wasn't really allowed in there without him. "It might be dangerous," he said.

You didn't have to tell me twice. Danger was my middle name. I snuck in whenever I could.

That was if I could get past Humphrey. Humphrey was the Professor's talking cat. Yes, I know you're not going to believe me but it's true - this cat really did talk.

A lot. I never found out how the Professor trained him. He said that if anyone discovered the secret, they would take Humphrey away to dissect him. As annoying as this cat was, I didn't really want this to happen.

"Max, come and look at this," the Professor said one day after I dropped round with the usual chocolate cake. I'd been hassling him for ages about travelling to Mars, maybe seeing my Martian friends. I was going through a pretty tough time at school, teachers getting on my case about daydreaming. And then being beaten up by Murky the big fat turkey as I liked to call him. But only when he wasn't around. So I thought I'd be better off with a group of aliens.

The Professor went into his study and came back with a large roll of paper. He pushed the teacups, the chocolate cake and Humphrey off the dining table. Humphrey screeched and landed on the floor with a thump.

"Sorry, Humphrey," said the Professor, "but I've got something important to show Max."

"Oh no," said Humphrey, slinking out of the room, "here we go again."

"Now here," said the Professor, unfolding his drawing, "is a new propulsion system I've been working on. This will propel a spacecraft into space at 290,000 kilometres per hour. That's ten times the speed of - what was the name of that thing that used to go into space? Oh yes, the Space Shuttle. This one will travel 7 million kilometres in a day!"

He did some quick calculations. "Let's see: Mars is around 55 million kilometres from Earth, so it should take us 8 days to get there."

"How does it work?" I asked. I prepared myself for a long explanation.

"Well, it's really quite simple," said the Professor and he held up a jam jar. "Inside this jar I've built a plasma generator."

I didn't let the jam jar faze me. "What's plasma?"

"Plasma is ionised gas which is another way of saying the gas is magnetised. You know what magnets are, don't you?"

Magnets attracted things made of certain types of metal, I knew that. But I still couldn't see how the stuff inside the jam jar could move a spaceship.

"See," continued the Professor, "here I've put the solar cells and the solenoid coils. They act as a switch like the ignition switch on your car. And you know that solar cells can be heated by the sun - that will be our energy source. These solar cells and the solenoid coils will create a dense magnetised plasma."

I kept on nodding. It was better that way. Once the Professor got started, you just had to let him finish.

"The plasma which, remember is now magnetised, will inflate an electromagnetic field 16 to 20 kilometres in radius around the spacecraft. This electromagnetic field will catch the wind from the sun. Do you know about the solar wind, Max?"

I shook my head. The sun had wind? Yeah, right.

"Well, the solar wind is a powerful stream of charged particles travelling at 1.6 million kilometres per hour. So, if you can catch this wind and get it to push you, you can travel pretty far."

"How far?"

"All the way to Mars."

Before I could let this sink in, the Professor had jumped up and started pacing the room. And talking to himself. He often did this and I wasn't too worried. Not just yet.

"You know," he said, sitting down again. "I think we might even get there in one and a half days."

I tried to get him back on track. "But what does the solar wind have to do with this jam jar?"

"Well, the electromagnetic field created by the plasma chamber in this jam jar will act as a huge sail and catch the wind. Like a sailboat does. What we'll have is a spaceship with a very large sail made up of all these charged electromagnetic particles."

"Would it really work?" I thought I should ask.

"Oh yes. There's enough power in the solar wind to move a little spaceship about six and a half million kilometres in a day. Of course," said the Professor, looking thoughtful, "it needs a bit of work. At present, it's only a jam jar."

I was glad to see he'd got a grip on reality so I left him to get on with it and headed home. After Mum made me take out the rubbish and Dad gave me the usual lecture on homework, I escaped to my room. I got out my telescope and tried to find Mars. The telescope was a present from Uncle Septimus. My parents didn't like me watching TV or spending too long on the Internet. A telescope however was considered 'educational' - you can imagine how popular I was at school. But I got my own back on them: I actually preferred the telescope.

There was an orange, reddish ball low down in the sky. I was getting goosebumps just thinking about going there. What would it be like? I knew 'red' didn't mean 'hot' - it meant reddish dust storms. And there were those polar caps, like the north and south poles on Earth. The Professor had said they were made of ice. He'd seen them getting bigger in winter and smaller in summer so maybe they had seasons on Mars, too.

I'd read about the atmosphere on Mars - mainly carbon dioxide, very little oxygen. Not healthy. And it would get down to minus 87 degrees centigrade at night and not higher than minus 5 in the day! So, not much sunbathing then. That was cold enough to freeze carbon dioxide and anything else left outside, like fingers, toes, cats. A good excuse not to take Humphrey. I was really more of a dog person anyway. Except my dad wouldn't let me have a dog.

It was sort of ridiculous when you came to think of it. I mean, there'd been 30 missions to Mars, looking for water or life or whatever, and they'd all failed. What made the Professor think he could do this?

I stayed up quite late watching Mars, turning rusty red, shadows playing across its surface. Mum looked in on me, told me to get to bed. Then I dreamed about it - and the Martians. I woke up shaking. But I was desperate to go and willing to give the Professor the benefit of the doubt.

## II
## Hatching a Plan

There was a lot of doubt in my mind when I arrived at his house after school. For a start, the Professor was nowhere to be found. And Humphrey had disappeared, too. He was always left on guard duty on the porch; the Professor naturally worried about his inventions being stolen. Don't let that sleepy cat fool you! Humphrey can wrap himself around your ankle with jaws of steel.

Then I heard gurgling noises from the garage. There were also puffs of smoke and a smell like socks left under the bed too long. I peered in through the window. The Professor was in his white lab coat sending sparks through the jam jar. Or several jam jars judging by the mess on the floor.

Humphrey was catching mice in the corner. Nothing keeps him away from his food.

I pushed open the door. The Professor was perched on his workbench. He looked up, sheepishly, and apologised for the chaos but he'd been doing some tests. His long, grooved face had more craters than the Moon. I gathered he was depressed so, to cheer him up, I asked him how long it would take to build that plasma-thingy-sailing-spaceship. It did the trick.

"You mean, the Solar Breeze?" said the Professor. He always had a name for his inventions. It was usually

19

the first thing he invented. "Well, I've been thinking. A few days ago I heard from a former colleague of mine, Professor Mustelid. We lost touch when I was, er, when I left the Department and she went to - somewhere in Asia. A brilliant scientist." He seemed lost in thought.

"Anyway, she's back now - oh yes, she's a woman." He stopped. "Does it matter?"

I shook my head. It wasn't that I thought all scientists were naturally men, but Uncle Septimus knowing a woman! I was still smiling when he continued.

"Professor Mustelid is also researching electromagnetic fields and she would like to get together. Do stop smiling, Max." I tried but I couldn't. "Anyway, she's managed to procure a small spaceship which she needs to get rid of. It's taking up room in her garage and she wants to move her car in there. Although why people would want a car when they could have a spaceship…"

"But that's fantastic!" I interrupted. "That means you can put the plasma sail on this spaceship!"

"Certainly. We just need the right conditions. Well, that will actually be more difficult. I'll need to build an ionising chamber and I don't really have the equipment here." He surveyed the glass and smoke.

"The Institute does," said Humphrey, who was sunning himself on the window sill and keeping a lookout for any mice making a dash into the garden.

The Professor shook his head. "I can't go back there. They've forbidden me to set foot in the lab ever again."

"Why?" I asked. No one had ever told me the reason Uncle Septimus had been asked to go "on extended holiday".

"Oh, some little problem," the Professor shrugged. "Just because I wanted to make the cleaning lady's vacuum cleaner go faster and make tea at the same time."

"Well, you did give her a fright," said Humphrey. "She wasn't expecting to be chased by a vacuum cleaner spurting tea everywhere."

"Oh, I admit there were one or two problems to iron out but that was no reason to ask me to leave. Especially since I was getting on so well with my other research. Although some people were rather worried about it," he added sadly.

I thought a bit, then said cautiously, "This is going to work, isn't it?"

"Of course it is! We got you to the Moon, didn't we?"

I nodded, trying to feel convinced.

"If we can think of another way to test the plasma generator," continued the Professor, scratching his chin. It looked like he hadn't shaved for weeks. As usual.

"Well," continued Humphrey, "we could break in and use the lab at night."

Both the Professor and I looked at each other. "That would be highly illegal," said the Professor, but he was smiling.

"Has that ever stopped you before?" asked Humphrey.

The Professor's smile got bigger. "Hmmm. And Anna - Professor Mustelid - has returned to work there. So, we'd just be assisting a colleague in her research." He jumped off the bench, looking a lot younger than his sixty-two years. "Let's get this mess cleared up. I'll call Anna and ask her to meet us at the lab tomorrow night."

# III
## The Break-in

Well, it was difficult to sneak out of the house but I managed it. There was this trellis outside my window, nice and sturdy to hold all the flowers my mum intended to plant. Except she never got round to it. The trellis needed to be strong because I was a bit on the pudgy side. Which is why Murky kept picking on me. And why my dad wanted me to do more sport.

I made it to the Professor's round midnight.

"Is your woman friend meeting us there?" I asked him.

Humphrey sniggered and the Professor blushed. "She is not my woman friend," he stammered. "Well, yes, Professor Mustelid is a woman and she was - is - a friend but she is also a very learned scientist."

"Okay. Is Professor Mustelid going to meet us there?"

"Yes, we've arranged to meet at the side entrance by one o'clock. That's when the security guards take a break so hopefully we can get into the laboratory without being seen."

I saw him looking at me with a worried expression. "Maybe I shouldn't take you with me, Max."

"Are you kidding? We're a team, Professor. There's no way you're leaving me behind."

"Me neither!" said Humphrey. "I remember those mice in the medical lab." And he licked his lips.

We set out for the University on the other side of town, travelling on the Professor's tandem, pedalling as fast as we could. Humphrey was in the basket, looking suitably scared.

When we reached the lab we made our way round the back of the building. There, waiting for us, was a red-haired woman, very thin, very tall. I must say I didn't like the look of her. She was too skinny for a start. And she had a long, thin mouth. Her lips looked like they were painted on; she obviously wasn't used to smiling. She briefly flashed one at "dear Septimus". Blink and you would have missed it.

I obviously didn't rate one. She nodded in my direction when the Professor introduced me but I caught the look of annoyance that flickered into her eyes. I couldn't get the colour - puke-green, I think.

"We have to hurry," Anna said, as we entered the building. "The security guards come around every hour. I don't want them to find me - us here." I did wonder then why she seemed so nervous.

Soon we were inside the lab which contained the particle accelerator and the ionising chamber. There were consoles and vats and tunnels, it all looked like a giant warehouse.

"Here, Max, I want you to hold the jar," instructed Professor Boggle. "Professor Mustelid and I will start up the chamber and control the charged particles. When I give you the signal, I want you to pour the plasma gas from the jar into the opening here and then close the door and stand well back. You, too, Humphrey."

"Why do we have to stand back?" I asked.

"Because if you don't, you might be blown away by the force of the wind which we are going to try to create inside the tunnel."

"Okay. Humphrey, stay with me," I said, taking hold of the jar and looking round for the cat who had gone in search of mice.

"I'm over here," called Humphrey from behind a desk. "And I'm busy!"

"Quiet!" shushed the Professor. "We don't want anyone to know we're here. I'm going to start the generator now."

Suddenly I heard footsteps behind me. I froze. What would happen to us if we were discovered? What would my parents say?

Then a small voice said, "Aunt Anna, where are you? I'm getting bored."

I turned around to see a little girl with black pigtails and one tooth missing, smiling up at me.

"Hello," she said, "who are you?"

"I'm Max," I hissed. "Go away!" That's all we needed right now - a girl spoiling everything.

"Milky!" You could tell her aunt was even more annoyed than when she'd met me. "I told you to stay in the car!" It was like silent shouting. Made me shiver all over. "Never mind now. Stand behind him", jabbing a finger at me, "and keep quiet!"

Milky did as she was told, although 'quiet' wasn't in her vocabulary. "My name's Milky. My daddy's abroad.

So's my mummy. I'm staying in England with my Aunt Anna," she said brightly, as if I cared.

"Milky?" I whispered. "What sort of a stupid name is that?"

"It isn't a stupid name," Milky whispered back. "My daddy's an astrophysicist and he named me after the Milky Way - the constellation of stars in the sky," she explained as if I didn't know. "Because they're so beautiful."

Actually that was a nice thing for her father to do but, of course, I didn't say so. She soon started up again.

"What are you doing? Is it important?"

"Yes," I replied. "Very important. So don't get in the way!"

She looked like she was about to cry. "I can do important work, too. My mummy's a scientist and I used to help her before she went away with my daddy. I want to help Aunt Anna but she always says I'm a nuisance."

I was beginning to agree with Aunt Anna. "Well, I help Professor Boggle and he's more important." Since that wasn't going to shut her up I added, "Besides, he's a man."

"So? What can a man do that a woman can't?"

"Lots of things," I said, although I couldn't think of any. "Important things."

"Like this?" she asked, pointing to my jam jar.

"Yes!"

"What are you going to do?"

"Pour this jar into this hole when the Professor gives me the signal."

"Is pouring a jar into a hole important?"

"Very important!" I tried to make myself look taller.

"Oh, that's easy," said Milky, shaking her pigtails. "I can do that!"

"Max," the Professor's voice was coming through the intercom. "I'm going to give you the signal soon. When I count to three, I want you to pour the plasma into the hole, close the door, then you and Milky stand clear. Understood?"

"Understood, Professor!" And I got into position.

"Right. Counting down. One."

Just then Humphrey came strutting round the corner with a juicy mouse swaying in his mouth. Milky took one look, let out a scream that could split eardrums and grabbed my arm.

"Two."

"Don't do that!" I cried, trying to hold on to the jam jar.

"Three!"

I just managed to pour the gas into the chamber before Milky fell against me. A whoosh of air came out of the hole, throwing me, Milky, Humphrey and the mouse across the floor. I was still holding the jam jar.

"Are you children all right?" asked the Professor as he ran out of the control booth. We'd been blown clear across the room.

"It was her fault!" I shouted.

"No, it wasn't!" cried Milky. "The mouse scared me!"

"Not to worry," said the Professor, picking us up. "We've managed to do our experiment. Now I think we'd better get home. The next shift will be along any minute now."

We managed to get out of the building without being seen. The Professor had Humphrey firmly under his arm, Aunt Anna was dragging Milky along and throwing me dirty looks.

"We'll meet tomorrow at your house, Anna," the Professor said as we got on our tandem. "And see if we can't fit this propulsion system onto your friend's rocket." I saw him put a large canister into the bicycle basket. Humphrey didn't look too happy perched on top. We waved but Professor Mustelid was already in her car, screeching off down the road.

# IV
## Introducing the Skycar

The next day, Saturday, I made up some story for my parents about being invited to a birthday party at a school friend's. As if.

They were desperate to believe it so they dropped me outside a house round the corner from the Professor's. I waved until they drove off, then raced over to his house. We got the bus this time since Professor Mustelid lived in the next town, or rather up a hill off the main road.

Her house was old, too, almost as run-down as the Professor's but not as welcoming. In fact, rather spooky. She met us at the front door before we could even knock. "Come this way." No "hello, how are you?", so we followed her. There was no time to stop or say,"Nice place you've got here." Just as well. There was nothing warm or friendly about it. We passed a kitchen, I think, but it only had a sink and a microwave. I did notice there were computers in every room and cameras up in the ceilings.

Professor Mustelid clip-clopped down to the basement. "My laboratory," she said, pointing to more computers, long metal tables, vats, test tubes, freezers. Professor Boggle looked impressed but it didn't occur to him to ask - as I would have done - why she needed a lab at home if she had one at the University. Or did she? She kept saying he could come and work there any time he wanted. She put her beak-like nose close to his cheek; it made my skin crawl.

We climbed up some other stairs to a backyard surrounded by a high wall. In one corner was a decrepit old building, almost falling down. No car was ever going to be safe in there. But inside was an amazing vehicle: like a racing car, wings out the back and side but bigger, about three times the size of my dad's BMW.

"It has an ion-jet engine which can do 80 km/sec and it can take off vertically," announced Anna.

Wow! Every boy's dream rocket.

"Did you design this, my dear?" asked Professor Boggle.

"Ah, no. A friend. He's letting me use it."

"But are you sure your friend will allow us to put a solar sail on it?"

"Oh yes, he has no need of it. Now." I thought it strange that someone who had designed a flying car would want to give it to Professor Mustelid. Especially when she wanted to get rid of it.

But Professor Boggle was rubbing his chin and saying, "Well, I think we can adapt it. Yes, I can see where we could mount the plasma chamber, here, and we could put the ioniser there. Then the sail comes out the back once the engines are turned off." He went round the dream machine explaining to Anna how it would work.

Meanwhile, I looked around the garage. Just the usual junk - similar to my dad's. Except for a strange-looking globe with tubes like spider's legs. One of them started moving towards me. I backed away but it twisted around my arm, pulling me to an opening in the side. The door creaked and out popped Milky. "Hello!"

I must have been frowning - this girl spelt trouble - for she added, "Aren't you glad to see me, Max?"

"What are you doing here?"

"It's one of my daddy's inventions - a recycling bin. I was picking up rubbish. Oh, sorry, not you, Max!" She giggled, then looked over at the two professors and lowered her voice. "I always hide in here when Aunt Anna's in one of her moods."

Just then her aunt's voice shot over our heads. "Milky! What did I say would happen to you if I found you in here again?"

I thought I'd better defend Milky who was retreating back into her globe. "She was just showing me around."

"And you," Professor Mustelid jabbed me. "Should know better!"

"Anna?" Professor Boggle came over and put a hand on her arm. "I think we should have a look at the drawings I've brought."

"Right." She flashed me a dirty look. Her speciality.

We went back inside, into an even more uncomfortable room. I sat on a black leather sofa. It wasn't like the squishy one Professor Boggle had or the chintzy, flowery ones my mum preferred. Because it was a hot day, my legs stuck to it. It was painful having to peel them off.

Milky was telling me that her father was a scientist, too, and all about her family but I wasn't really paying any attention. I was still trying to peel my leg off.

Aunt Anna was making more of an effort now. "Would you like something to drink? Or to eat? She smiled, sweetly. That was almost scarier. "Hugh Mungus!"

"Bless you!" I said.

The smile disappeared. "I was calling my housekeeper. Ah, there you are, Hugh."

The room darkened as a large figure filled the door frame. "Hugh Mungus looks after me," she explained. "And keeps house."

I couldn't imagine anyone less likely to clean and cook. He had huge arms and a long moustache which hung down both sides of his mouth. This made up for the lack of hair on his head which was shaped like a bullet. An enormous bullet. His hands were like pieces of steak. I didn't want to check out his feet.

Milky was inching her way round the back of me. I was guessing they didn't hit it off. "He's scary," she said softly. I caught a look, his eyes seemed to be everywhere.

Hugh brought us tea and rice crackers. "We get lemonade and chocolate cake at Professor Boggle's," I whispered to Milky.

"Bad for teeth," hissed Hugh Mungus. He had ears everywhere, too.

"Come and look at these drawings Professor Boggle has made," Anna was saying to her housekeeper, if that's what he really was. "Hugh takes an interest in all my work," she explained when she saw the Professor's surprised look.

I wandered around the room and left the adults bent over the drawings and calculations. I knew Professor

Boggle would tell me eventually what we'd be doing but I felt in the way now. Milky joined me.

"I'll show you something secret," she whispered, pulling me round a corner and out of a door. We walked down a white corridor and into another white room. "Look in here. What do you think those are?" The place was filled with low light and at least ten tanks.

"They're fish. So what?"

"Not just any fish. Special fish. I heard Hugh Mungus tell Aunt Anna so. He called them fugu but she calls them puffer fish. She seems pleased to have them."

"What do they puff? Cigarettes?" Fish weren't really my speciality although these looked sort of interesting - white with a black eye mask and black mouth. Right now all I was concerned about was how we were going to get to Mars. And when.

Humphrey slid in, I'd forgotten about him. "Any mice in here?" he asked. "I've been all over this house and it's impossible. Much too clean. Even the basement. Hey!" He spied the fish tanks.

"What have we here? Come to Daddy, darlings." Besides mice, there's nothing Humphrey likes better than a big, juicy fish. These fish were definitely on the plump side. And getting plumper.

"I don't think we should be here," I said, suddenly nervous. "Humphrey, get your paws out of that tank. You might - oh, you have." That stupid cat!  He was holding a fish between his claws, a fish which was ballooning in size.

"Wow! I've died and gone to heaven!"

"Oh dear, I don't think Aunt Anna will like this," said Milky as Humphrey chomped away on his jumbo meal. Suddenly he seemed to freeze. He'd eaten half his puffer fish but wasn't moving anymore. The balloon fell into a squidgy mess at his feet and his rigid body keeled over on top of it.

"Help!" shouted Milky running from the room. "Humphrey's dead! Humphrey's dead!"

I poked at the cat. Like a furry rock. I tried to move him off the soggy fish. His eyes were blinking, in panic, but the rest seemed paralysed.

The door burst open and in ran the two men and Anna, dragging a crying Milky. The Professor picked up Humphrey, dangled him upside down, twirled him round his head. But he was still stiff.

"I think I'd better get him home quickly," he said. "I'll call you tomorrow, Anna. Come, Max. Take my bag." We hurried out of the room. I stopped to pick up the briefcase and heard Anna ask Hugh, "Which one?"

"Number two. Our best one."

I raced down the hill after the Professor. "Is Humphrey going to be all right?" I panted.

"If we can make him sick and cough up whatever he ate." He was slapping the cat on the back but it was like pounding wood. Except for Humphrey's bulging eyes there was no sign of life.

"I wish he hadn't eaten that puffer fish," I shouted.

The Professor stopped dead. "Puffer fish? Do you mean fugu?"

"I think that was the name."

"They're highly poisonous. What was Anna doing with puffer fish? But that helps me find an antidote. If we can keep him going for twenty-four hours, he'll be all right."

The bus came and somehow we got the frozen cat back. I don't mind admitting I felt like crying. The first thing the Professor did was go into his medicine cabinet and get castor oil and pour it down Humphrey. That did the trick. The cat was sick all over the floor. Then he went sort of floppy. But at least he was breathing.

Professor Boggle told me to get on home, my parents would be worried and make enquiries about this birthday party. I hated to leave, not knowing whether Humphrey would pull through, but I headed off. I tried to convince my mum I'd had a good time but she could tell by my face that I hadn't. I just said I'd eaten too much cake. She said, "Well, what you need is a nice bit of fish. Dinner's almost" But I threw up before she could finish.

# V
## Caratacus Gets Involved

On the following day the flying car arrived at the Professor's house. I'd dropped over to check on Humphrey who was chasing mice and swearing off fish for life. It was getting dark and I knew Mum would have kittens if I was late again for supper, so I said goodbye and opened the front door.

A low-loader was just pulling up with the rocket on the back. Hugh Mungus got out and Professor Mustelid ran past me, and into the house. She asked Professor Boggle where his garage was, where should they leave it. He came out and the three of them managed to get into the wooden structure at the end of the drive. They started mounting the propulsion system almost straight away. The Professor was already calling it the Solar Breeze. And laughing with Anna, thanking her for making his dreams come true. Oh, yuck.

I thought I'd be in the way again so I left. I looked in the cab of the truck but couldn't see any sign of Milky. They must have left her at home, she wouldn't like that. I did spy a small pink suitcase with flowers. Which made me see Hugh Mungus in a new light.

I couldn't get over to the Professor's for a few days. Dad was home from one of his sales trips and this called for 'quality time'. We went to the cinema, kicked a ball around and he asked me if I'd like to go to summer camp.

Oh sure, get picked on by even more sporty kids. But I said, yes, I'd love to. I had a plan.

When I finally did get to the Professor's, there was nothing left to do. He'd mounted the ioniser and the generator that would eject the electromagnetic sail. But he also had a container with another sail. It was amazing stuff! So airy - it just seemed to float off my hand when I touched it! And it twinkled and sparkled. The material was reflective, you see, and when it caught the solar wind, photons of light from the Sun would bounce off the sail, doubling its power. We'd be able to go twice as fast! A hundred and sixty kilometres a second! The sail was going to be huge - once we got it unfurled - about 40km across. Mind-boggling. And I hadn't even known!

But we were having trouble persuading Caracatus to move on board. I haven't mentioned him, have I? Well, Caracatus is the Professor's talking computer, a real grumpy so-and-so. If you call him a 'machine' or 'it' instead of an 'intelligent life form' he has a hissy fit. But we needed him to control the rockets, calculate our trajectory, angle the sail - complicated stuff.

"Please, Caracatus," said the Professor trying to flatter him, "we need you to release the electromagnetic field to catch the solar wind. You have to judge precisely when to do it, at what angle and then set a precise course for Mars. So you see, it's very sophisticated and a great responsibility. And, only such an intelligent being as yourself can do it."

"Granted."

"Please, Caracatus," I added when the Professor winked at me, "we need you, you're the best."

"You're just saying that because you want something." There was a long silence. "But do you ever come to see me? Do you call? E-mail?"

"Ah well, Max," said Professor Boggle, looking serious. "We'll just have to use Professor Mustelid's computer." He was smiling at me as he said it.

There was some serious whirring and whooshing going on in the circuits. "What? No doubt an inferior model!"

"But if you won't do it, Caracatus?"

"Who says I won't? Take me to this contraption."

The Professor and I carried him into the garage, placed him inside the Solar Breeze and let him get his bearings. It took a while - you can't rush an artist like Caracatus - but after a suitable spell, he agreed to be our onboard computer. Phew!

Professor Boggle then acquainted me with all the workings, the communication equipment, data-storage system. I'd already been going over the Professor's drawings with him but now I really felt like part of the team.

"Professor, you know the holidays are coming up. Dad wants me to go to summer camp and I was wondering if you could tell him I was going to science camp. And you'd be one of the counsellors."

"And it would be somewhere far away?" I was watching for a reaction. "You know, so I could go with you to Mars."

His sideburns twitched as he looked up from adjusting the computer's circuits. "But of course you're coming with me, Max. I couldn't go without my best assistant." That's why I liked Uncle Septimus, he always took me seriously. No one else did. "Oh I see, we need a story for your parents. Yes, I suppose they would look askance at our leaving Earth. Well, I'm not opposed to telling a little white lie. Shall I say you could come to my Space Camp?"

See? That easy. No fuss, no "you're not old enough for this." It was settled and he squared it with my parents. I don't know how but they seemed happy. And when your parents are happy, you don't ask questions.

There were two more days to go before school was out and I was going to 'camp'. I went over to the Professor's that night, needed to check some things with him. Walking up the drive, I noticed a light bobbing up and down in the garage. I crept up to one of the windows and looked in. Someone was prowling around the Solar Breeze! And the lock on the door was broken! Mum's uncle may be odd but he wasn't likely to break into his own garage. Then the doors opened and our ticket to Mars was inching out, like someone was pushing it from behind.

You know how you react sometimes in a split second? I picked up the nearest object, an old tyre iron, and waited. As the figure came parallel with the door, I raised the tyre iron - and fell over backwards. Well, it was heavy! But I'd managed to scrape his head for I heard a yelp as he sat down sharpish. I didn't stay around to see who it was. I ran into the house, tripping over Humphrey who had heard the commotion, and into the Professor who was just coming out.

He saw the Solar Breeze in the drive and gave a shout and shot something into the air. I found out later it was his portable cannon. It did the trick. Whoever the criminals were - there seemed to be two of them running off - they weren't going to hang around for more of the same.

We pushed the Solar Breeze back into the garage and checked for damage. Nothing. Who would have wanted it? This was no ordinary vehicle; you weren't going to go bombing down the motorway in this baby. Although you'd have fun trying.

I could see the Professor was rattled so I got permission to spend the night. Before I went to sleep I asked him if he knew anyone who would want to steal the Solar Breeze. He took a long time to reply, "No, no one I can think of." But he sounded worried.

# VI
# Saying Goodbye

We borrowed Mum's car the next day to take my stuff over to Uncle Septimus and to say goodbye to Anna. There was no telling how long we'd be gone and she hadn't been too specific about what she was going to be doing.

But when we reached Professor Mustelid's house there was no sign of life. We knocked, we shouted, we tried looking through windows. Nothing. The garage was the weirdest: completely empty, cleaned out. Clean even.

"Maybe she's gone to get her new car," I said, unconvinced.

"Maybe," was all the Professor would say. Again in that worried voice. "Perhaps we should try to have a look inside."

Well, that wasn't going to be easy but I had under-estimated my great-uncle. He pulled out a series of keys and was just trying number three when the door opened. We both took several steps back as the imposing form of Hugh Mungus appeared. He was wearing a bandage on the side of his head.

"Professor Anna not in," he announced sternly.

I thought my Professor showed great presence of mind for one usually so absent-minded. "Not to worry, Mr Mungus, we'll wait." And ushering me in, he pushed past the surprised housekeeper.

We sat on the black sofa, the Professor was here to stay. I must admit I admired his cool under Hugh Mungus's penetrating stare.

I pointed to his bandage. "What happened?" His eyes darted fireballs at me. He moved closer in a manner I didn't like.

"Hugh!" Anna's voice made us jump. She was barking at her housekeeper as if he were a trained dog. She motioned him to the back of the room.

"I'm so sorry I wasn't ready to greet you," she purred. "I had a headache. Hugh had orders - instructions not to admit anyone."

"We've come to say goodbye, my dear," said the Professor, rising. "Mars is at its closest alignment to Earth. We leave day after tomorrow."

"So soon?" I thought I saw her grow paler than she already was. "You know, Septimus, I've been thinking. I should really go with you. My research requires a more in-depth acquaintance with the geological structure of Mars. Besides you need an assistant. Someone to look after you." She was standing close to him now, stroking his arm. My stomach turned, not just with the fear that I wouldn't get to go.

"That's very kind of you, my dear." Oh great, he was weakening. "But I've got Max to assist me."

Good old Professor Boggle!

She gave me one of her classic looks, like I was a particularly repulsive insect. "I'm sure Max wouldn't mind. Would you, precious?" She gave my cheek a pinch which was going to leave a red mark for days.

"Where's Milky?" I asked, rubbing the raw skin. I moved further into the sofa.

"Gone. Back to her mother."

"Milky told me her mother was abroad, with her father. I don't think she would have gone without saying goodbye."

Anna's beak-like nose came close to mine. "You are a nosey little boy, aren't you?"

I tried to lighten the mood. "Not a patch on that hooter of yours." Didn't seem to do the trick.

The Professor sought to save the situation. "I have a wonderful idea, Anna. Why don't we rig up a communication centre here and I can keep you informed of all our movements? And I'll be bringing back samples which we can analyse when we return. In fact, I was hoping to collect some minerals for the University."

She made a sort of grasping motion with her hand. "No need. I mean, if you bring all the minerals to me, I'll make sure the Department gets them."

The Professor wrote down some co-ordinates for her and they discussed frequencies and computer programmes. I asked to use the toilet. Hugh, who was taking notes, pointed down the hall.

I thought I'd take a look round. It didn't make any sense, Milky leaving in such a hurry. She'd told me her mum would be away all summer until she had to go back to boarding school. And there was that pink suitcase.

I found the room with the puffer fish. Yup, they were still there, bobbing about. And a trunk in the corner which I hadn't noticed before. I couldn't resist a peek. A large, black-haired doll was lying underneath some clothes, blue eyes staring right through me. Then I realised whose eyes those were. Milky's! I felt for a pulse. No, not dead. Not even stiff. But that weird look that Humphrey had had. Panicked.

What to do? Well, it was stupid and if I'd had time to think I would have seen that. But I dug her out and lifted her over my shoulder. I stumbled down the corridor, past the door to the front room and called out, "I'll wait in the car, Professor." I heard, "Righto, Max", but luckily nothing else. No heavy footsteps behind me.

I got through the door, climbed carefully down each step, juggling the sack that was Milky. I opened the back of the car and sort of flopped her in. She rolled on the floor. Good, that way I could cover her up with the blanket.

I didn't have that long to wait. The Professor was coming down the steps, accompanied by Aunt Anna - some aunt. But not Hugh Mungus. What if he went into the puffer fish room and discovered it was minus Milky?

"Come on, Professor," I called from the car. "I've really got to go. Again." I waved to Professor Mustelid. "Bye! Thank you for having us." Over the top, I know, but I was dead nervous. She was looking more than her usual unpleasant self.

I was quiet in the car, trying to work out what to do. If I told the Professor that I'd kidnapped Anna's niece, he might make me take her back. After all, Milky could have been hiding in that trunk. No, not with that look - that fugu look.

"Professor? What did you give Humphrey to make him get better? After he'd eaten the puffer fish."

"Why do you ask, Max?" The Professor was looking at me sharply. "You haven't eaten any, have you? Oh no, you were out of the room at the time."

"What are you talking about?"

"Hugh Mungus offered me some sushi - you know, raw fish - while you were in the toilet. By the way, you were gone a long time? And I'm convinced there was some fugu among it. Luckily I managed to put it in my pocket when they weren't looking."

I swallowed hard. "Do you, do you think they were trying to poison you?"

"Why do you say that, Max?" We were just pulling into his drive.

"I've got something to show you," I said and pulled back the covers from Milky.

He didn't look surprised. "I was afraid of this. Help me get her into the house."

We put her in the upstairs guest room, next to the one I always had. She was still staring. Humphrey looked in, sniffed and raced out again, tail between his legs. The Professor had me get the castor oil, ladled it down her and made her be sick into a bowl I was holding. Not a nice sight before lunch.

But she still didn't respond. At least her eyes were closed and she seemed to be sleeping, so we let her be. When we were downstairs I asked the Professor if she'd be all right.

"I'm afraid Anna's turned her into a zombie."

"What!" He'd been watching way too many horror movies.

"She's given her just a little fugu, enough to paralyse her reactions. She'll be able to respond to commands."

"But why?"

"That's what I don't know. What has Milky told you about herself and her family?"

"Not that much. She goes to boarding school here in England. She came to spend the summer with her aunt. But…"

"Yes?"

"Well, she said, 'I'm staying with Aunt Anna. She told me Mummy was abroad with Daddy.' It seems odd that her mother wouldn't have told her herself."

The Professor stroked his whiskers. "Yes, it is odd. Very odd."

"Oh yes, and her dad's a scientist but Milky doesn't seem to know where he is."

"Yes, I knew her father at the University. A very unusual physicist. But then he…" He looked out the window and was silent. "Well, we've got no choice. Mars won't be this close to Earth for another fifteen years. We don't want to miss our window of opportunity." He was pacing the room now. "But I've got no proof."

"Proof of what?"

"What? Oh sorry, Max, I was thinking aloud again." He resumed pacing. "Your parents are going on holiday tomorrow, aren't they?"

"Yes, the moment I leave for 'camp'. Oh, Dad said you told him I was going to Sports Camp, not Space Camp,"

"Did I? Oh, I may have. You know how I hate speaking on the telephone." He gave me a knowing wink.

"I thought it would be easier that way. But that still leaves us with the problem of Milky." He came to sit beside me. "I think the only thing we can do, Max, is postpone this trip. I know you're disappointed." I was. "But we need to make contact with her mother. I have some friends who may be able to help us. And there's a few more days left. We might still make it."

Or not. It didn't seem fair. I knew this girl spelt trouble the moment she crept up on me. But she was only eight and we couldn't leave her with an unstable relative and a scary housekeeper.

"Come on, Max. Let's look over the map of Mars and imagine what it's going to be like."

He got the drawings out of the safe and spread them over the table. I never tired of looking at the Valles Marineris and the Elysium Plateau and Olympus Mons, the largest volcano in space. I'd never get there now. All because of some… girl.

"You know," said the Professor, "it's amazing how lucky we are on Earth, considering our atmosphere." He saw my puzzled look. "If you think of a football with a layer of paint around it," he explained, "that's the atmosphere around the Earth in scale terms."

He continued, because he liked to. "The early Martian atmosphere was affected by solar radiation and one and a half billion years ago it evaporated away. There's only thirteen per cent of it left, frozen at the poles. Now its atmosphere is one-hundredth the pressure of Earth's, cold and barren with super-sized dust devils, one kilometre in height. Huge dust storms can cover vast expanses of the planet and last for two months." Was he trying to put me off?

I turned to the diagram of the Solar Breeze. Then I remembered Hugh Mungus's bandage. I looked at the Professor. "He was the one, wasn't he? Last night in the garage."

He smiled at me and nodded. "Both of them."

"But what did she want it for?"

"What we want it for - to get to Mars."

"Why?"

He tapped his pencil on the table until I stopped him. It was getting on my nerves. "I don't know how much to tell you, Max. It could put you in great danger."

I could feel the excitement rising. Fear, too, but mainly excitement. "You can rely on me, Professor. We're a team, remember?"

"Yes, I know, but I've been sworn to secrecy. It doesn't matter by whom. You must promise not to tell a soul about this, Max." I gave him my word. "Professor Mustelid used to be a brilliant scientist, in physics as well as in chemistry. We often worked together, Milky's father, Anna and I.

"But then she became obsessed with discovering a new element which she'd identified from the last space probe. You remember the one that hit the asteroid and brought back samples? It was a very hard element, harder than titanium, and she wanted it to be named after herself: 'mustelidium'. Well, no one accepted this. She became very bitter and went abroad. That's the last I heard of her until she resurfaced here."

"What's the connection with Mars?"

"That's what I can't figure out. She was never keen to come along until today. I assumed she was merely being helpful when she offered me the rocket. She knew I was working on a new propulsion system - had been for a long time." He was looking into the distance now, almost sadly. "She's changed since coming back. And she doesn't work at the University, I've checked."

"I was wondering about that. But won't she be able to make a plasma propulsion system, too. Now that she's seen you do it?"

"But it's no good without the photon sail. And she doesn't have the formula for the material. It's reflective, a carbon-fibre backing. I was able to make up a length in my workshop and get a friend to produce the quantity I need."

He must have seen my head steaming as I tried to work it out. "You see the electromagnetic sail - from the plasma - is only the one sail. The second one is the photon sail. She doesn't have the plans for that one. And that one will get us to Mars faster."

"And that's why she wanted to steal the Solar Breeze - to get the photon sail?"

"I wonder whether..." The Professor was going off again.

"What?"

Just then the phone rang. While the Professor went to answer it, I checked up on Milky.

She was gone! Window open, bed empty. I looked out, over the roof into the garden. No sign anywhere! I tried not to panic, not to think of Hugh Mungus lurking in the dark. But when I got back to the living room, it was a job to say who looked paler.

"Milky's gone," I said, wondering if the Professor had had bad news too.

He raced outside instead of going upstairs. I thought I'd better follow but by the time I reached the garage, he looked like himself again. "The Solar Breeze is all right," he said, inspecting the craft.

"But Milky's gone!" Hadn't he heard me?

"I know, Max. I was afraid she'd been programmed to damage the Solar Breeze."

"You mean - deliberately?"

"Well, remember she's been turned into a zombie. She may not realise what she's doing."

We combed the garden and the neighbourhood for her. I went home, said goodnight - and goodbye - to my parents. They were off to Hawaii the next day. I was off to - nowhere. I couldn't sleep. I dreamt of Anna and Hugh Mungus and Milky - she was screaming. I got up, dressed, left a note to say I was off, early, to the Professor's. What did it matter?

When I got there, I let myself into the garage. It struck me that I hadn't seen Humphrey all evening but that wasn't unusual. Being a cat, he was contrary. As only cats can be.

I looked at the Solar Breeze, silver, shiny, rockets ready for firing, plasma sail and photon sail mounted. It just didn't seem right that such a lovely machine should be stranded in a wooden shed. I climbed in. No good moping, let's pretend we're really going! Here were the provisions all ready for taking - dried food, powdered drink. Right next to the space suits. Didn't think much to the irradiated smoked chicken or the dehydrated green beans but it was bound to taste yummy in space. And then, when we got to Mars…

It was no good, I couldn't make myself feel better. I sat down and jumped up again. A ball of fur had clawed its way up my back! "Watch it, buster!" shouted Humphrey.

"Hey! Ouch! Where have you been?"

"Watching your girlfriend."

"What? Who?"

"Milky. She's over there." Wedged between Caracatus and a cupboard full of food and drink lay Milky, snoring softly.

"I saw her climb out the window upstairs and down the roof - I had a hard job keeping up.

"She was looking for something. And she found it."

Suddenly the door was yanked open. "Who's there?" came the Professor's deep voice. Before I could tell him, there was a streak of pigtail and Milky flew out of her corner, straight into Professor Boggle. She caught him right in the stomach and knocked him backwards onto the console. Out cold. Humphrey had had enough excitement for one night and darted out the hatch.

# VII
## Take-off

Great! What was I supposed to do now? One unconscious Professor, one deranged girl - with scissors. With scissors! What on earth was she doing with those? She was coming towards me, pointy tips foremost.

"Give me the sail. I must have the sail. Cut piece. Take back to Aunt Anna. Give me the sail."

This was freaking me out. She was talking in this mechanical voice - like a robot. I'd seen old movies about what you were supposed to do when women went crazy. But I wasn't about to slap Milky when she was looking to cut me open.

I lunged for her hand, squeezing it tight so she would drop the scissors. It was amazing how strong she was! She clawed at me, kneed me, then pushed me against the console, too. Whoa! I could feel something knob-like in my back, several knobs. A dull roar juddered through the spacecraft. I was thrown forward on top of Milky, the scissors were flung down the end.

I scrambled up, hanging on to the console. Milky looked pretty lifeless spread out on the floor but I couldn't worry about that - I had a runaway spaceship to deal with! The Solar Breeze had already crashed through the garage doors and was gathering speed down the drive. I climbed into the seat and studied the dashboard. No, nothing like a car, but I remembered enough of what the Professor had taught me.

I switched on Caracatus. "About time, too," he hissed. "Do you know what you're doing?"

"No, and I need you to help me. So stay cool." I should talk. The Solar Breeze streaked across the intersection at the bottom of the road. Luckily no cars this time of morning, just Joe Hickory out walking his chihuahua. Ran off shouting and waving. Both of them.

"Time to ignite rockets," said Caracatus. "Shall I proceed?"

Right. Crunch time. I can do this, I told myself. "Go for it, big C!" I shouted, throwing caution and everything else to the wind.

The whoosh that nearly split my eardrums and the force that pinned me to my seat was better than any ride at Disneyland. I heard Milky, sliding down towards the back and hoped she wouldn't impale herself. But didn't much care right now. I could see that the Professor was wedged between the seat and the console and still breathing. So he was okay.

I wasn't. Despite Caracatus taking control, I was as scared as I'd ever been. Not even Murky could have terrified me any more. My house was disappearing below me - the house I should have been fast asleep in. Then my school - no great loss - then my whole town. The woods, the fields, the motorway, the river over the hills. Hey - this was pretty amazing! I could see huge cities looking like Lego and the mountains, that my dad had always promised we'd get to some day. It was like a geography lesson - only in 3D.

When the Professor finally woke up, we were in the stratosphere. He was relieved to see I'd programmed in the coordinates for Mars. But not surprised. Now my dad would have been because he thinks I can't do anything right. But not Uncle Septimus - he just accepts.

I filled him in. "Well done, Max. Now, let's see if the photon sail has suffered any damage." He worked his way down the back - we were just beginning to get weightless - and checked first on Milky. She seemed to be in a deep sleep, so he made her more comfortable. That's when he noticed the little bit of reflective material she was clutching.

"Oh dear, I see she's managed to snip a piece off." The container had been opened, some of the sail had spilled out. "Just a small corner. Should be all right." Hopefully. "Let's get the electromagnetic sail going, then we'll see how much power we have."

Not before time, Caracatus informed us. The plasma tanks were running near empty, time to jettison those. "Could we have them land on Murky's house?" I asked. No answer from Caracatus. Guess computers don't know what it's like to be bullied - and to want revenge.

I tried to look out the windows when I wasn't double-checking instrument readings. It was really the most stupendous view! We saw North America and South America pass underneath, surrounded by the Atlantic and Pacific oceans. And Africa looking incredibly huge! Tucked in the corner was Australia and New Zealand, down at the bottom Antartica - it made me shiver just seeing all that ice and snow. I thought we could even see the Great Wall of China!

"Look, Milky," I said, trying to raise her up. "That tiny speck is England. And Africa is coming up."

I thought I detected a twitching but her eyes were still glazed over.

"Let her rest, Max," said the Professor. "She's had a bad knock and she needs to sleep it off."

Then I remembered. "What about your phone call? Who was that?"

He finished programming Caracatus, gave him his daily dose of praise and sat down beside me.

"You deserve the truth, Max. And what you're getting into. The call was about a friend, the one who made the photon sail. He's been poisoned."

Oh. Now was not the time to tell me this. "Who - what did it?"

"Well, my contact seems to think it was - fugu." He nodded. "And," he added, looking just a bit worried, "Anna and Hugh Mungus have disappeared."

"Is that good?"

He was studying the console intently. "Anna was working on nuclear-powered spacecraft. Something Milky's father had invented - before he disappeared last year. We - that is the Government - think they, that is Anna and her organisation, may already have a nuclear-powered spaceship. That's why I wanted her to stay in touch with us on our mission. I was hoping we could find out what she was up to. And where Milky's parents were."

"When you say the Government, do you mean…?" He nodded. Wow! My uncle was a spy! Not an absent-minded professor but an honest-to-goodness spy! Wait till I told the kids at school.

But I was forgetting something. "And a nuclear-powered spaceship would be - bad?"

"It would go very fast. Faster than the Solar Breeze."

So that would be 'bad' then. Very bad.

# VIII
## An Exciting Voyage

The next day - or night - the Professor was getting ready for our landing on Mars. He figured the answer to Anna's strange, not to say dangerous, behaviour must lie on Mars. It might have something to do with 'mustelidium', the material she discovered in the asteroid samples. Asteroids were zipping around the solar system every day and - yikes! - that one was close!

Anyway, the Professor had me clear stuff away, tie things down, including Milky. She was still a bit dazed and bumping into the controls - and we weren't happy about that.

Whenever I passed a window, I shot a glance outside. I never tired of looking out at the blue and white globe disappearing astern. Earth looked like a fragile beachball - one kick and it would deflate. Surprising why it hadn't already. It had suffered quite a few knocks in its time floating through space.

"Professor, why do you think we abuse the Earth so much?"

He smiled, and shook his head, almost sadly. "Yes, it's a puzzle, Max. Something so delicate, so wonderful. But we're always confronted with choices. Whether we save our planet, or destroy it - it's our choice."

"Why would anyone want to destroy Earth?"

"Greed - people always wanting more, never being content. Valuing material possessions above clean water, clean air, stupendous scenery. Unwilling to share the Earth's valuable resources with others - feeling they have to have a larger share." He continued to look back at the object of our affection. "Just look at it, Max. In this vast darkness, isn't it the most beautiful, the most precious thing we have?"

No argument there. So, before I started wondering why I wasn't down there, I turned round to see what we were heading towards.

"Professor, I think you'd better see this!"

Coming straight for us and gathering speed was the biggest rock I had ever seen. It was leaving a trail of something white and icy-looking behind it and I knew it had to be a comet. But knowing that wasn't making me any calmer. Surprisingly, the Professor was.

"Oh yes, I had a feeling we'd be meeting up with that. The Oort Cloud occasionally spits out a few. No problem is there, Caracatus?"

"Affirmative. Trajectory will pass within 99.4 metres. You should detect a slight vibration." Just then the Solar Breeze lurched, before righting itself. Caracatus knew his stuff. The comet sped off, blue and yellow tail streaking across the sky.

Milky was surfacing. She yawned, stretched, looked around - and started crying. Typical girl, couldn't take the strain.

The Professor went over to comfort her. I was still smarting about those scissors.

"It's all right, my dear. You're safe with us. Do you remember anything that's happened?"

She wiped her nose on the back of her hand - yuck! - and said slowly, "I remember Aunt Anna shouting at me. Then she made me eat some fish. Said it would do me good. I remember Hugh Mungus laughing. I was so scared." She started trembling which sort of got to me, so I went over to, well, pat her hand. "It's okay, Milky. They can't get to you up here."

"Where are we?"

"We're in outer space." Her eyes grew wider.

"We're on our way to Mars," I said as if it were the most natural thing on Earth. Or in space.

Her eyes were really bulging now. And she started shaking again. "Aunt Anna was talking about this. About the Solar Breeze, how she had to have it. And I was supposed to do something for her." She started sniffling.

"The photon sail," I prompted before the Professor could stop me.

"That's it! She wanted me to bring her a piece of the sail."

"Yes, you nearly did. And a piece of me, too." Okay, it wasn't nice but you've never been face to face with an eight-year-old zombie with scissors!

"That's all over now," said the Professor soothingly. "Let me make some chocolate milk. That will calm us down." He went off to fiddle with the microwave he'd built into Caracatus.

"Why did your aunt want to get the photon sail?" I whispered.

Milky shook her head. "She didn't tell me. But I think she wanted to get to Mars, too. I saw her looking over the maps with Hughie and she said, "We must get one for our rocket."

"Your rocket?"

"Yes, my dad made two. But I never saw the other one."

"I thought your dad was abroad?"

"He was. I don't know where he is now." Her lower lip was wobbling. "And now Mummy is gone, too."

"But you said - she was abroad, with your dad." Why didn't people stay put, or get their stories straight? Much less confusing.

"That's what Aunt Anna said when she collected me from school and brought me to her house. But," she looked up at me with those big blue eyes, "do you think Mummy's disappeared?"

I didn't know what to think but there was definitely something fishy going on. And it wasn't just the puffer fish.

"Drink this hot chocolate," the Professor was handing us each a sealed container with a straw. We didn't want hot globs of liquid floating past us. "And then strap yourselves up in these sleeping bags. We've got a long day and night ahead of us."

I helped Milky on with hers and then did up mine. As I dangled from the supports, I looked out the window at the pinpricks of light speeding by. What had the Professor once said? "We are all made of stardust." Two hundred billion stars in the galaxy, fifty billion galaxies. No point counting them all. I'd be asleep before...

I had the weirdest dream that night. But then I woke up and realised it wasn't - a dream, or weird.

Don't panic, I told myself. This is where you wanted to be. The Professor was still asleep but Milky was up watching the stars whizzing past the telescope window and the Earth growing ever smaller.

"Come look at this, Max," she whispered. I saw a large red object growing brighter and brighter.

"Wow! Is it Mars already?"

"I don't think so. It's probably a novae, a new star. They get brighter as they form."

"Really? I knew that." Well, I wasn't going to let on, was I? "Let's tell the Professor."

He was awake instantly and seemed to know where we were. What's more he looked happy to be there. But the novae didn't occasion the same excitement in him as it had in Milky and me. "Oh dear."

"What?" I'm not good on 'oh dear' first thing in the morning."

"It's not a novae - it's a supernovae, a red supergiant. And it's collapsing."

"Oh dear!" Now Milky was getting in on the act.

"Would someone please tell me why I should be worried!"

"A supernovae is a collapsing star. It collapses because of gravity, when the core can't support the outer layers. Its brightness can increase sometimes by 16 magnitudes."

"What does that mean?"

"As bright as a 100 million stars put together."

"No, I mean, what does it mean for us? Is it dangerous?"

"Oh yes," chorussed the Professor and Milky. Great. All this time the spaceship was filling up with a light so blinding that I had to put on my sunglasses. "But it's nothing to worry about." What part of 'dangerous' wasn't I understanding?

"You see," the Professor was now programming Caracatus with new coordinates to change the angle of the photon sail, "because of our reflective material, we may speed up." He was rubbing his hands now. "The more light the sail reflects, the faster we'll go!"

"You mean we'll get to Mars quicker?"

"Yes, but we'd better sit down and fasten our seat belts. Quickly now."

We weren't quick enough. The ship shook and surged forward as if a giant hand were pushing it. I flew past my seat, past Caracatus who was whirring away, and tried to catch hold of Milky who was bouncing a bit herself. I just managed to hang on to my sleeping strap but felt like a spider dangling on its thread. Flashes of lightning were whipping past our window along with shiny dust particles like millions, billions, trillions of tiny stars.

Milky had caught up with me. "Isn't this fun?" she shouted. I was wondering if she'd been at the puffer fish again. She clung on to my arm and said cheerily, "I wonder if we'll get sucked into a black hole."

Nice way to cheer me up. "Well, we'd just get out again. Wouldn't we?"

"Oh, we might get out, but we wouldn't be arranged in the same way. Our arms might be on our heads and our toes on our noses. All our molecules would be broken up and re-arranged." She was really loving this!

The Professor interjected. "No need to worry. There are no black holes in the vicinity. Besides a black hole only happens before a supernovae explodes, not after. We would have been in one by now." Well, that was showing her. "But take a look to port."

There was a red ball coming towards us surrounded by a pinkish dust cloud. I couldn't make out many details, only occasionally some bulges, dark splotches, what looked like rocks. We had reached our destination.

# IX
## Arrival on Mars

"We'd better circle one more time," said the Professor, "until the dust storm has cleared. I want to aim for the East Basin, it might be safer than the Valles Marineris. Not so many canyons to get snagged on."

I could see the poles, white against the red landscape. As we got closer, Olympus Mons, the largest volcano in the solar system, came into view. Then the Tharsis mountains. We were aiming for the north, for the Arcadia Planitia. It looked like a flat plain, not too many boulders, no craters, and sounded nice. But from what I could see, it wasn't worth getting excited about. Imagine a huge reddish-brown toad, covered in warts. It gives you some idea.

We were still hovering, trying to find the landing site, which was tricky because of all the dust devils. They would just erupt out of the surface with no warning. One minute calm, the next - poof! - this whirling red tornado. And the dust storms could last for weeks, apparently. I'll never complain about rain again.

"It's no good, Max," said the Professor, "we're going to have to chance it. Let's get Caracatus to pull in the photon sail. We'll float down on to the surface and hope we're in the right place."

"Does Caracatus know where we are?"

"Oh yes," the Professor said confidently, then whispered, "but between you and me, neither one of us has ever done this before." Like this was going to make me feel better.

We came down in concentric spirals, through the sandy haze, swaying a bit too much for my liking. I wish I hadn't had that thermo-stabilised brownie for dessert. There was a final wobble, then 'kerplunk' - we'd landed.

It was sort of anticlimatic. Pretty exciting getting to Mars and all, but now what? All I could see outside were boulders, sand dunes, some mountains and canyons in the distance and red dust everywhere. It was way dustier than my bedroom before I'm forced to clean it.

The Professor took a deep breath. "Well, here we are. I think we'll take a look outside, shall we?" He reached into a cupboard underneath his seat. "First things first: spacesuits. Max, get into yours. Milky, here's one for you."

I looked at him. "How did you know she'd be coming?"

He smiled. "It isn't exactly a suit - more like a bubble. To bring back any samples. But it's insulated against the cold and radiation and I can attach this oxygen filter on to the outside. Now I want you, Max, to make sure it doesn't become detached."

It was tricky getting into the suits. The Solar Breeze was pretty well designed and most of the time we'd been either lying down or sitting up - or floating from cupboard to console. But putting on bulky thermals required a lot of clever gymnastics. And then we put

Milky into her bubble. She was giggling so much that I had to tell her to keep quiet and stop wasting oxygen.

We opened the door carefully and climbed out. When I heard it close behind us, I suddenly realised how very far from civilisation we were. And I don't mind admitting, I felt really lonely. Although the Professor and Milky were with me, around us was nothing but black space and empty desert.

Or so I thought. Now you're going to find this hard to believe and I kept pinching myself to make sure I wasn't dreaming - which is pretty hard to do when you're wearing a spacesuit - but stay with me. Down on the ground, at my feet was a large golf ball, then two of them, rainbow-like. I hadn't gone very far - it was difficult with Milky. I could have rolled her along but I didn't want to knock off her breathing box. The Professor had already jumped several feet ahead - he was really getting into the whole low gravity thing. I was doing little bunny hops and feeling stupid. Then I saw these golf balls.

Funny pebbles, I thought, and kicked one. They both vanished below the surface, as if sucked into the ground. Weird, but I didn't want to lose sight of the Professor - he was heading towards the edge of a canyon - so I jumped a little higher. Which got me a lot further. I could see by Milky's expression that she was having the time of her life.

All of a sudden, right in front of me in the dust popped these huge, glassy eyes. And I crashed into them!

The momentum spun me head over heels. I let go of Milky in her bubble and she went floating off.

The Professor had disappeared over the ridge. When I came to a stop, I realised I was holding Milky's breathing apparatus. If I didn't get it to her double quick, she was going to be vaporised toast! But where was she?

I heard the Professor's voice in my earphones. "Max, where are you? Is Milky all right?" Then he cut out. I tried to call him up but my communication system was dead, too. Now was the time to panic.

And I did because just then a metal cylinder shot up beside me. A panel slid open and out rolled Milky. She was still breathing, smiling and pointing back to the opening. The cylinder was waiting. Going down? So down we went.

# X
# Underneath Mars

Once below the surface, our elevator turned into a glass compartment so we could see where we were going. Past what looked like solid sheets of ice, past rock walls with waterfalls. We reached a platform overlooking a large hall which seemed to go on forever.

A huge city lay beneath us. There were tall columns and round globes, vertical cylinders and horizontal cylinders. In the rock walls were openings which looked like caves but had windows and doors. In the middle of the hall was a huge lake with fern-like plants round the edge.

I rubbed my eyes or rather the visor of my space-helmet. All that dust must be making me see things, I thought. But it was still there. I looked at Milky and she was just drinking it in, mouth open, eyes bulging. Speaking of which: I haven't mentioned the inhabitants. They were tall, slim, covered in silvery grey material. Their legs looked sort of bendy, their arms more like those of an octopus. The most noticeable thing was their eyes: big and bulging, the ones I'd run into. Sorry about that; I tried to look contrite. Judging by the fact that no one had attacked us yet, I must have made a reasonable impression. One of them looked familiar. The Professor, minus spacesuit, was striding towards us in the company of a sleek silvery individual. He seemed to be sharing some hilarious joke.

"Max! There you are! And Milky! Come and meet our friend, Oog. I think you two know each other, don't you, Max?"

And now it's confession time: Oog - and Zoog, Moog and Oogli Woogli - were the Martians I'd met on the Moon. See, I told you you wouldn't believe me.

Oog touched my helmet with his head and said "Welcome" in a mechanical sort of voice. It turned out he could speak many Earth languages because he had a small voice-activated computer which translated our speech into Martian and vice versa. I was speechless. Milky, too. First time for everything.

"Take off your spacesuits," the Martian said, "we have an oxygen-rich environment. We will now go to my pod." He led us onto a moving walkway and we positively zipped along. We passed other Martians who smiled and waved and saluted Oog. I guess we had the head Martian with us.

We arrived at a globe-like building and Oog spoke to one side which opened. We moved through and waiting for us were two more Martians, one about Milky's size. Oog introduced Moog, his 'life-partner', and Oogli Woogli, 'our clone'. A cute little fellow, he came up and touched Milky and then hid behind Moog. They both had translator boxes, too. "What is that?" he asked, pointing to Milky.

She looked annoyed. "That's a girl," I said, smirking.

"Female!" said Moog. Pointing to herself, she smiled and said proudly, "Me, too." Milky reached out to stroke the little Martian who then said he liked her even though she was human. Which was pretty big of him. Of course, they remembered me from the Moon so we caught up on old times.

The Professor and Oog were talking excitedly about the amazing -ness of it all. I mean, our being on Mars and the Martians actually being glad to see us. He said they'd observed the previous attempts with great hilarity on their 3D-screens. Nobody could believe our amateur equipment. But Oog said everyone on Mars reckoned we'd get there one day, we'd just have to evolve a bit more.

"Have you ever been to Earth?" I asked.

"Oh yes, many times. Some have welcomed us - but some have reacted very strangely, imprisoning our voyagers and experimenting on them." He shook his large, angular head.

"Very barbaric." He and the Council were delighted to see real humans. They felt there was now scope for meaningful interaction.

Oog and the Professor started talking technical so I joined Moog and Milky in the kitchen where the female Martian was programming "sustenance". The counters were gleaming and there was no mess anywhere. When Oogli Woogli spilt some liquid, the surface immediately sucked it up. This place had Good Housekeeping written all over it.

"Come and see my living space," said the little Martian and he pressed a button in the wall and we were in another room. Two computer screens and straps on the wall were all I could see so not really my sort of decor.

But there were pads on the floor which, when pressed, would fold out into a comfy chair or a trampoline-like bed or even a climbing wall. And then fold back again if you no longer wanted them. "Clean your room!" was not a problem here!

Oogli took me over to his computer. He put a helmet on my head with goggles and, before I could protest, I was actually in the screen! He must have pressed several buttons at once for I was driving a car one minute, flying a plane the next and diving underneath the ocean before I fell exhausted to the floor.

Moog came in and scolded Oogli in Martian - a succession of high-pitched squeals which would have made me behave in no time. "Time to digest," she said and ushered us into the eating space.

A large table and stools rose out of the floor and we all sat down. We were served by small robots who kept ferrying between the cooking area and us. In our honour we were given Earth food although they may have got the nationalities confused. It was a mix of Chinese take-away, pizza and traditional English cooking which actually turned out to be delicious.

We were encouraged to discuss - not like at home where my father still felt that kids should be "seen and not heard" and preferably neither. So I asked, "How do you get oxygen? I always thought the atmosphere of Mars was made up of carbon dioxide."

"That is correct," said Oog, "but we have developed a system for creating oxygen by heating and cracking the carbon dioxide into oxygen - which we breathe - and carbon monoxide which we use for fuel and power. The methane in our atmosphere is also used to power our heating and ventilation systems. After our digestion, we will show you."

"Do you have any pets?" asked Milky. Oogli couldn't find the word in his computer but Moog explained that there were no animals on Mars - they would take up too much oxygen. But they did have nine million species of insects. Not very cuddly, though.

We left the robots to do the dishes and stepped onto the moving walkway again. Oog pushed a button and we zipped along the top overlooking the lake which was fed, we were told, by the ice caps. They were minus 150 degrees centigrade at the Poles! Shiver time!

Turning a corner, we travelled down an escalator and came to a large, glass-covered globe. There were hundreds of these all around the lake and in the middle connected to all the others was a green sphere, like the hub of a giant airport.

Inside the first one I couldn't help noticing how warm it was and how many different plants there were. "A part of our biosphere," Moog explained. "Here we have tropical plants: palm trees, orchids - the sort that grow in your southern hemisphere."

"And we get oxygen from our plants!" piped up Oogli, eager to show off what he knew. "And from our waste. The rest we use as fertiliser."

"Yes, and we have different spheres for different ecological zones. A wide variety of flora," added Moog, who had waited for Oogli Woogli to finish speaking.

"How do you manage to grow so many plants," asked Milky, "when you don't have any sunlight?"

"As you have noticed we have lots of carbon dioxide in our atmosphere which plants like to breathe. We pipe it down with the water from the permafrost crust above us to grow all this."

All we could say was, "Amazing!", "Fantastic!", "Unbelievable!". Then we saw a few more biospheres before heading back to the pod.

Oog and his family invited us to stay with them in their guest quarters. They had the Solar Breeze put in an underground garage to protect it from the dust storms and introduced Caracatus to a couple of super computers, so he was happy.

When I went to bed that night, I didn't know what to make of it all. And I had some really bizarre dreams. They started out scary - falling into black holes, being disassembled. But then they'd always turn out all right. In the morning Moog said that she'd turned on the dream machine which ensured that all my dreams were pleasant ones. And were recorded in case I wanted to watch them again.

After what I think was breakfast, Oogli Woogli introduced me to his friends. Luckily they all had translator boxes, too, and some were even my size so I didn't trip over them. I was really impressed by how nice these guys were. They kept asking me all sorts of questions about where I came from and what I liked doing: they made me feel real important. And best of all, they didn't pick on me because I was chubby or different or on Oogli Woogli because he was small. They could have taught my school a thing or two.

Milky wanted to stay behind with Moog - I think she was missing her mother - so it was a boy-and-Martians-only day out. We zipped along the walkway, down to the lake. They had me paint myself with waterproof body paint - like wiping yourself all over with jelly. We were going swimming, I thought, but then out came these boards. Okay. Surfing, but on a calm lake? Didn't think this would catch on.

Then someone switched on the wave machine and we were really bombing across. Up to the top of a huge wave, crashing down into the valleys. You know I'm no good at sports, at least everyone says I'm not, but this was exhilarating! I was getting to the other end of the lake in no time. So I flipped round on the board and surfed back, dodging the other boards, swishing in and out. There were all these Martians gathered on the side, applauding me. It was magic! I had no idea I could do this! It just goes to show what the Professor has always said - you don't know until you try.

By this time the Professor and the others had joined us. I could tell that Milky wished she'd come surfing, but apparently she'd learnt all about Martian cooking and mixing chemicals to create some interesting food. So, time not completely wasted.

We had a picnic in one of the biospheres - the tropical rainforest. Amidst the singing of mechanical birds, the melodic splashing of waterfalls and the perfumed smells of multicoloured flowers, we had soya. Not as bad as it sounds and the surroundings made up for it.

I was admiring Oogli's suit - very cool rainbow colours which kept changing depending on his body temperature. A beeper sounded on his bottom telling him his suit was about to inject his vitamins.

"Aren't these smart textiles amazing, Max?" asked the Professor, who was like a physicist in a particle accelerator, jumping about excitedly. "They self-wash and self-repair, too. I never could get mine to do that."

Moog offered to make me a suit, too. Or would I rather have a tube of insulated body paint? "Any chance of body paint which would make me invisible? There's this bully I'm anxious to avoid."

She said they had scientists working on it but there was still some debate about whether it was ethical or not. "But if there is a problem with someone, we try to resolve it by talking, by trying to find a compromise."

Meanwhile Oog was looking intently into his glasses. I noticed the tiny computer screen. "You must excuse me. I have been reminded of a very important meeting. Perhaps Professor Boggle would like to attend?"

No doubt about it. The Professor put on his jet pack and they were off. "And we will take a little trip to the southern hemisphere," Moog suggested. "Would you two enjoy that?"

Milky and I nodded. "But isn't that pretty far? How long will it take?"

"For your spacecraft it would take one day. But we will teleport. It will only take a few minutes."

"What's teleport?"

"Oh, I forgot, you have not developed that on Earth yet. But you know about quantum physics?" Oh sure. "You can transfer your atoms from one area to another by light particles." Do it all the time.

I remembered Milky's description of a black hole. "We'll be put back in the same order, won't we?"

Moog made rapid hiccoughing noises which I took for laughter. "Of course! We are very developed here. We have not had a misalignment for many eons. Now where has Oogli Woogli gone?" She tapped into a directional sensor on her glasses which showed her his location. "Ah yes, Bio Beach. He likes to work on his tan."

We collected him on our way to the teleporter. I was a bit nervous about all this scrambling of molecules and atoms but it was a new experience. And I was always game for new experiences.

We entered a round chamber with pulsing lights. "I will just program our destination," said Moog, pushing buttons. "Now stand close to the wall and hold on tight." Numbers streaked across a screen and lights flashed up and down the wall. I felt a tingling all over which only lasted a few seconds. Then the lights stopped, the door opened and we stepped out into a completely new world.

"How did we do that?" I asked, picking Milky off the floor. I was checking my arms and legs just to make sure they were in their usual alignment.

Moog and Oogli didn't seem the slightest bit fazed. "We travel through wormholes using photons of light," said Moog.

"Light travels at 300,000 km/sec," chirped Oogli who had figured out that we were easily impressed.

"And," continued Moog, "we use the teleporter to travel on the ripples of light."

"Your atoms were scrambled and then put back together!" Oogli again.

"I figured that out," said Milky, just a little miffed. "It's like going through a black hole."

"Not quite," Moog reassured us. "The same information in your atoms is sent by quantum particles to another point in space and time. Then here you are! It is perfectly safe."

"But black holes are not," piped up Oogli. I did a double-check of all my appendages.

The southern hemisphere was much rockier than the north. We had a great view of the Valles Marineris and the Tharsis Mountains; they'd built a glass dome to take advantage of the view. Off in the distance was Olympus Mons, 25 kilometres high, you couldn't miss it.

Waiting to greet us was another member of the family, Moog's "biological sibling", Zoog. Apparently he was a well-known scientist who was developing intergalactic space flight. He had even been to Earth. He said how nice it was to see me again - we had already met on the Moon - and that he'd been convinced I'd eventually make it to Mars - which was more than I had been!

"Let us have a look at the Museum of Earth Objects," said Zoog, and we entered a cylinder which looked like it was filled with junk. "Our voyagers have collected these from the Moon and from the surface of our own planet. It is part of our 'Keep the Universe Beautiful' campaign." We stepped onto walkways which took us round the exhibits. There were lots of Martians, pointing at the metal objects, sometimes laughing, sometimes shaking their heads. Lots of old spacecraft, lunar buggies, bits of satellites, robots - an amazing amount of rubbish.

"There's Rover!" I said. "I was wondering what had happened to him."

"Yes," said Zoog. "He was sent to our planet to look for minerals and decided to stay. He is much happier here, playing with the other robots." And indeed Rover was wagging his tail, rolling over and begging for scrap metal from the junior Martians. If NASA could see him now.

Somebody was saying something to us and we asked Zoog to translate. He seemed reluctant but Oogli Woogli jumped right in. "He said that you Earth people should not keep sending junk up into space just because your planet is so polluted."

"It is not your fault, dears," Moog hurriedly reassured us. "Your civilisation has not developed the technology to get rid of your rubbish. You will in time."

"Before it is too late!" interrupted Oogli. "You will drown in it if you do not!"

I couldn't agree more but we were all beginning to feel uncomfortable so I asked Oogli if he'd like to come to visit us on Earth. Oogli Woogli shook his head and said he'd never want to leave Mars, given the state of the Earth. Moog tried to shush him but said the feeling was Earthlings didn't like Martians.

"Why?" asked Milky and Oogli together. Moog and I looked at each other. Then we looked at Zoog. How were we going to answer that one?

"Sometimes people are scared of those who look or act differently," Zoog started.

"And they're not too bright either," I carried on. "It makes the dummies feel good if they can beat up someone who's not like them. For some reason the really stupid people think - if they think at all - that people who don't share their looks or interests or language or whatever are inferior. And that is supposed to make them, the dummies, superior. Which it doesn't. It just makes them stupider." I knew I was going on a bit - and probably losing them in the translation - but I felt strongly about this. From personal experience.

Zoog looked at me with interest and smiled. Moog and Oogli Woogli were nodding, thoughtfully. Milky wrapped her arms around them both and said, "We're all the same underneath." She had a real way with aliens.

"Let us have something to eat," said Moog. "You must be desirous of nutrition." She took some coloured tubes from a pocket in her, well, skin and gave us some Martian snacks. We couldn't really tell what was inside them - bright pink, green and orange but they were intriguing. One tasted like strawberries and oranges but another one like sausage ice cream. I didn't really want to know what they were made of although Oogli would have been very happy to enlighten me.

What I really wanted to know was where Martians went to school. Oogli looked puzzled. "What is school?"

"You know, where you learn things. An ugly building you go to five days a week. Like work."

"Oh, we are learning all the time. From our elders. And from doing."

"But what do you learn?" asked Milky. "Do you do maths and science and languages?"

"Everything," continued Oogli. "We learn by helping those who are wiser with the work that needs to be done.

When we are older we help our cities and then our planet. Everyone has a useful role to fulfil. Sometimes we train with our wise men and women if we are interested in their particular type of work."

"You see," said Moog, "Martian children are part of their environment. They, along with the adults, create it. We help our children to learn and we ask them what sort of world they want to live in. And we try to involve them in the decisions we make."

"Children are really very intelligent, you know," said Oogli, nodding wisely.

"That makes sense," I replied. "It's a bit like I'm learning about space from Professor Boggle."

Zoog agreed. "Wise men and women and children are very precious. It is a doomed civilization that ignores this."

We had a chance to look around one of the southern biospheres which incorporated the polar ice cap. Martians were skiing down the slopes, or rather sliding down on their elastic skin-suits. It looked like fun but we had to get back to our part of the planet.

We met up with Oog and the Professor at the teleporter and they arranged with Zoog to go on an "external expedition", which meant to the surface. Once they'd received permission from the Council. I was curious about why the Professor would want to expose himself again to minus 100 degrees. But we were due to teleport so I concentrated on my molecules and atoms, making sure I wasn't leaving any behind.

The next day Milky and I went with Oogli to his Centre of Learning which they attended when they wanted to top up their knowledge. The students sat on a cushioned floor next to individual computer screens. They attached a circular disc, which looked like a halo, to their heads.

"I wonder if they ever have a bad halo day?" I joked to Milky but she fixed me with a look - you know the kind - which told me to keep my smart remarks to myself.

There must have been 100 kids in that classroom but nobody was acting up and there was just a low chatter. The teacher appeared on the wall screen and the class applauded. Oogli told us that she was a scientist who was leading a mission to Saturn and Titan. She used the large screen to illustrate her lecture and asked the students to use their computers to work out trajectories to the nearest planets, length of time to travel and speed required. Serious mathematical stuff. Oogli was helping me and I was helping him and together we did quite well. At least the screen kept lighting up, "Well done!" which made me feel really proud.

One of the Martians sitting next to Milky seemed quite fascinated by her and was poking and pulling her pigtails. Suddenly his halo vibrated. The teacher was communicating with him. Whatever she said - or did - had a calming effect and the Martian returned to his computer screen. Nobody else noticed, nobody was distracted. Great way to maintain discipline. Wonder if I could use it on Murky.

We were sent out after an hour to one of the biospheres for the next lesson on cultivation. The instruction was to make notes on the plants that would be needed to sustain life on Titan, one of the moons of

Saturn, given its atmosphere. Oogli handed me a metal plate. "Just move your finger over the surface and the magnetic strips will pick up your brain waves."

"And do what with them?"

I could almost hear him sigh. Patiently he explained that the electric impulses in my brain would pass down my finger on to the surface. "All you have to do is think," and he smiled a little, "then move your finger and the pad will record your thoughts." Gosh, I loved this place.

We had a productive time in the greenhouse, literally. We grew corn and soya and beans and some fruit called 'ugli' - and it was. Then we went back to the classroom and compared notes and discussed what sort of ecosystem could be established on Titan. The teacher praised our efforts and asked us to write up a report which she would submit to the committee on Interplanetary Exploration.

"For real?" I asked, and was assured that, yes, all views would be taken into consideration.

"You know," said Milky, "I could really get used to being taken seriously."

Then the teacher asked for volunteers for the training mission to Saturn. Milky had to hold me down - I was itching to go. We finished off with Martian martial arts - Kung Jitsu - which is going to come in handy one of these days. I was doing pretty well until Oogli wrapped me up with his long tentacles and flipped me. He admitted he had an unfair advantage.

"Milky, Max, come on! Time for Astroball!"

We followed the students out to a large playing field with stools suspended round the edge. Lots of Martians were gathering, hoisting themselves up on the stools and moving through the stadium to their preferred position. I thought maybe Milky and I should grab one too, before they all hovered off, but Oogli and his friends took us over to a small hangar. "You two are on our team."

"But we don't know how to play - what's it called again?"

They looked at each other and one of them said, "Maybe they should be on the other team."

Oogli Woogli shook his head and opened a sliding door. "It is easy. You get into a small spaceship, see," and he pointed to a row of them, "they are what you call 'flying saucers'. And here we have an asteroid." He picked up a small, round rock. "And up there, do you see that big asteroid?" We looked up and saw a huge, rock-encrusted globe suspended in mid-air.

"Well, if you can make a dent in it with this little asteroid, you score a point."

"With you so far. But how?" There seemed a big gulf between me on the ground, holding little asteroid and big asteroid up in the air.

Oogli continued. "You bounce this one - the Astroball - off the sides of your spaceship, see here all around the edges. You have to keep the ball up in the air and fly underneath it to hit it. Come on, I will show you."

"It is a very popular game," said his friend reassuringly. "Sometimes we have competitions the length of the city - 3,000 kilometres. But try not to crash." Some reassurance.

We got into our flying bubbles. "Now, you push this stick down and the spaceship goes up," explained Oogli.

"And push up and it goes down. Left and it goes right, right and it goes left. Just think of the opposite to where you want to go." Oh yeah, like all the time.

Another friend patted me on the back. "You were great this morning at wave-cruising." I beamed. "Just remember, our best player is out ill so the whole team is counting on you." No pressure then.

I strapped myself in and tried to remember which way to waggle the stick. Above me Oogli was already soaring, dipping and diving. He could rotate his craft round and round, dribbling the ball off the edges. Milky was managing to pick up the Astroball, too, darting in under Oogli and bouncing it back to him off the end of her ship.

My turn. Left, no, right. Up, no, down. That was it, I was finally airborne. Suddenly I saw the Astroball steaming towards me. I tried to move my ship into position but the asteroid whizzed past. Oogli zoomed in to catch it and bounced it back to me by tilting his spacecraft to the side and flicking it up. I tried but wasn't quick enough and once again the ball just thudded off. I was also wobbling a bit and feeling queasy.

Meanwhile the other team had lifted off. They were cruising round us and 'now you see them, now you don't' was on the agenda. These guys were fast! And my team was relying on me? Well, I wasn't going to let them down! I pushed the stick fully down and whooshed up like a lightning streak. Luckily the asteroid was descending and I caught it square on the side and passed it to Oogli. He was heading towards the big asteroid bouncing the ball off his spaceship.

Milky was darting in and out, not really getting the Astroball, just getting in the way. I pushed my stick down to soar above them and get a better look. We were close to the goal now. I swooped down, just as the Astroball bobbed up and caught it on the front of the ship. By tilting myself at a 45-degree angle, I kept the ball going, scooting it back and forth on the edges of the ship until I was just near the big asteroid. Then, with one final slide sideways, I slammed the Astroball into the asteroid goal.

To my amazement and horror, the large globe which had looked so solid from the bottom, started to deflate just like a balloon being popped. "Well done, Max!" I heard Oogli's voice over my headset.

"But, but," I stammered, pointing at the disappearing goal.

"Oh, don't worry about that. It soon inflates again." And sure enough, when I turned back to look, there was the asteroid, suspended in air, as huge as ever.

After that it was a piece of cake. You could tell the other team was scared. They had obviously never seen an Earthling in action. I deflated two more goals, Oogli two and another striker one. It was a walkover. Milky did some nifty dodging and diving, confusing the opposition no end. We were the champions! And boy, did that feel good!

# XI
## More Exploration

There's nothing better than waking up the morning after with the sweet smell of success. It was a rare enough feeling, I can tell you. Moog, Oog and Professor Boggle had watched our triumph from their hover-seats and were just as thrilled as the three of us about our team's victory. We had celebrated well into the Martian night on Martian joy juice, which made us feel incredibly happy and incredibly tired. So we slept in. By the time we got up, the Professor and Oog had already set out with Zoog for 'External Exploration'.

I was a bit disappointed. Sure, I was having fun and the morning laser news featured a story on me, but I thought the Professor and I were a team. He usually included me in his plans, at least talked to me about them - which was more than my parents did - so yes, I was disappointed.

Oogli read my mind, which didn't surprise me. "We could follow them," he suggested. "I know where the external garments are kept - to protect us from radiation and solar flares. Much better than that flimsy material you arrived in. How about it, Max?"

I was up for it. "But what do we tell your - Moog? And what about Milky?" I didn't like her missing out on stuff. I felt sort of responsible for her.

"We will say we're on a field trip. We will take Milky with us."

They were in the southern hemisphere. Oogli transmitted ahead to say we were coming and a minute later our space scooter had pulled up beside their Mars Mobile. The Professor explained that the Council had given permission to extract minerals and take samples back with us. Oog and Zoog had kindly offered to show him - us - where to find them.

Dotted here and there were rocks of varying sizes so I assumed it would be no problem picking up a handful, putting them in our bubble bag and hauling them back. But I could tell the Professor was being very choosy. He was rejecting an awful lot, running a laser gun over them to check their mineral composition. Zoog and Oog were helping him while Oogli and I were playing Mars-tag with Milky. Not as easy as it looks in low gravity. At one point Milky, who was naturally very light, drifted off when a dust devil scooped her up. Zoog sent up a fibre-optic sensor which attached to her space-belt and anchored her to the surface. She was happy so Oogli and I left her floating there while we explored.

I was getting used to this landscape. It had a mysterious sort of beauty and more colour than you would think. There was the red and brown of the surface and the white of the polar cap in the distance. As the Sun rose, it turned blue - took some getting used to, I can tell you. The sky was butterscotch but if you got a strong wind, and we often did, it would turn red with the scattering dust. When we bounced down into a canyon, it was eerily black but the next second our rocket packs took us up on a ridge and we had a great view of the bright red soil and the far-away cliffs, the pinkish plateau and the pinwheel craters. Over the horizon were the moons, Phobos and Deimos, like two astroballs suspended in space.

We were in a rift valley which I learned later would have spanned the USA - the largest fault in the solar system. It was seven kilometres deep so we had a lot of fun, jumping down and then at the last minute turning on the rocket packs to zip back up again. It was minus 50 degrees and the atmosphere was pretty poisonous, but inside our spacesuits we were happy as rabbits. Except Mars didn't have rabbits. So maybe happy as the Martian worms we'd had for breakfast.

We were just sliding down some sand dunes when the call came to go back. They'd collected all they wanted so we hitched our scooters to the Mobile Unit and headed down the shaft to the dust-sucker which 'whooshed' us clean. Then over to the multi-garage where the Solar Breeze was getting an overhaul. The tear in the sail was being mended with extra photons and the ship was being fitted with plasma tanks for our return.

"Where do you get your plasma from?" I asked.

"From Jupiter."

"Say again?" I shook my translating computer.

"From Jupiter. You must come with us sometime. A fascinating place. We are sending a mission next month."

"But how?" both the Professor and I were gasping. This was defeating even his prodigious imagination.

"Jupiter is 90 percent hydrogen with a very powerful magnetic field. The plasma particles cling together and we scoop them up. Of course, we have a trading agreement with Europa, one of Jupiter's sixty moons. The inhabitants there are very warm." Zoog and Oog chuckled as if at some private joke. They explained that since Jupiter was this giant gas ball with masses of energy, naturally the inhabitants of any nearby moons would be very... Okay, I got it.

"Yes, Europa has claimed the rights to Jupiter. We understand the other fifty-nine moons are not too happy. Jupiter has a lot of gas and ice, so it is a good resource. Fortunately, they take our Martian food in exchange."

I wasn't quite sure who was getting the better end of the deal but it would have been rude to say anything. I would really have liked to accept their invitation, though. But maybe that would be stretching my summer vacation just a bit.

We went back for supper. A special treat, since it was our last night: red Martian slugs, sautéed in green algae. It wasn't as bad as it sounds but I was beginning to admire the Europa-ians. We got to stay up late since the Martian day is a half-hour longer than an Earth day anyway, and Oogli, Milky and I watched some transmissions from their satellites. It was cool seeing the different planets and galaxies, especially the Andromeda Galaxy with its huge black hole gobbling up everything. And we got to see a star forming in the Orion Nebula. It was like a giant furnace with white, blue, pink blazing clouds bubbling up.

But you can only take so much of Mercury's double sunrise and Jupiter's red spot and Saturn's rings. Milky had already dropped off and been carried to bed by Moog.

I said I'd turn in, too, and went to say goodnight to the Professor. I found him in his room, floating above a 3D image of the Solar System. I could tell something had been worrying him by the way his sideburns were bushing out. He's always pulling at those when he's got something on his mind.

"It's these minerals, Max," he confessed. "I'm worried about taking them back to Earth. They might fall into the wrong hands."

"You mean Milky's aunt?"

"Yes, and others. Even our government."

"But I thought you worked for them?"

He looked sad as if tussling with a great guilt. "Sometimes we scientists put our knowledge at the service of governments which don't govern wisely. As Anna has done. And I'm about to do." He got off his bed and started pacing the room.

"We say knowledge is power but it's no good without a clear conscience. And a sense of responsibility. Unfortunately, scientists can't always determine to what use our knowledge will be put. This mineral could be used for good. On the other hand it could produce a weapon capable of destroying everything - it's been tried before."

"But taking back a few samples wouldn't be doing any harm?"

"That would only be the beginning, Max. If we explore, we exploit. It will be like the Amazonian rainforest. Pretty soon, everything is destroyed, nothing is left for future generations to enjoy. If we've made it to Mars, others will follow if they think there is something to be gained. Would you want to see our friends' way of life eliminated? Mars may not look beautiful to us but it's their home."

Well, I thought Mars was great and I definitely didn't want it destroyed. But the Professor was off again. "That's why I left the University. If they thought I was just a bumbling inventor, they would leave me alone. Wouldn't pressure me to do work of which I didn't approve. I've only agreed to cooperate now because I don't trust Anna."

He was silent for a long time and I didn't want to break the spell. Eventually he sat down. "If we can no longer just wonder at the beauty and mystery of the Universe and appreciate its creation, we are lost." He shook his head. "No, we're not ready for this knowledge. Not until we're ready to take responsibility for our actions."

Well, I couldn't argue with that. I didn't want to. I wasn't about to cry either. I knew what we had to do: protect the Martians from ourselves.

# XII
## Time to Leave

I didn't say much at breakfast the next day, what with being sad and all. I'd made good friends and learned a lot - and had more fun than I'd ever had before. But there was the solar wind to catch and we didn't want to miss our opportunity to return home. And I was beginning to miss home.

I wanted to say, "Come and visit", but I thought if they did, they - and we - might be locked up.

Oogli was looking at me strangely. He was probably trying to read my mind and wondering what I was thinking. Milky was clinging to Moog and crying a little. It must have been tough on her, losing one mother, then her aunt turning her into a zombie. And now leaving your favourite Martian.

I could tell the Professor would have stayed. But he had a responsibility to get us back safely and, as he saw it, to make sure Anna and Hugh Mungus weren't causing any more mischief - and indigestion - with their puffer fish.

We said goodbye at the entrance of the cylinder. The Solar Breeze had been brought out and the engines were racing. They wanted to give us presents but the Professor was firm about not taking anything back except memories and not leaving anything behind - except footprints. I think Oog and Moog understood.

But Oogli slipped me a watch - it had a computer screen. "You can use it to signal. In case you want to come back," and there was moisture covering his protruding eyes. Milky hugged him, even I hugged him. Moog gave us a slurpy kiss and Oog touched our heads.

We entered the ship and lifted off. Caracatus, who had had the best time of his robotic life, set the coordinates for home. We waved and waved until the red dust of Mars covered our friends. And the blackness of space swallowed up Mars.

It was lucky that we left when we did because the solar wind was at its height and Solar Breeze fairly zipped along. It was logging about 1,000 kilometres a second! Even so, we were a bit subdued for the next few hours. I helped the Professor check the instruments and watched out for comets and asteroids. Milky sat by the window, looking miserable. I wanted to say something to comfort her, but couldn't. I'm not too good at that sort of thing.

But the Professor knew what to do. He sat with her, talked to her about the wonderful experiences we'd had, got her laughing. I was looking over at them, thinking how lucky we were to have Uncle Septimus with us and not Aunt Anna when all of a sudden our spaceship did a violent twist and started tumbling out of control. And I mean really out of control!

Anything that wasn't fastened down, flew up, down and around - including us! Milky landed on top of the Professor, I landed on top of her. We clung to each other and I don't mind admitting, I screamed as loudly as Milky. Only the Professor remained calm, calling to Caracatus to find out what had hit us.

But there was no answer. His circuits must have been knocked out, all we were getting was static.

Then flashes of light soared past our window, waves of the stuff. "Solar flares!" shouted the Professor and every time we got another flash, the ship would buffet and lurch and we'd be tossed like wet spaghetti.

Then, just as suddenly, the Solar Breeze righted itself and all was peace and quiet. Except for Milky sobbing and me about to join in. Caracatus came back online and informed us we'd just witnessed the biggest explosion in the Universe. Pass. "Ah yes, twists in magnetic pulses," the Professor explained. Double pass. I didn't really have the strength to take in yet another scientific explanation. I just wanted to curl up and sleep. Which I did.

Not for long though. The Solar Breeze was pitching a bit and it was clear that all was not as it should be with our ship. Even the Professor was now beginning to look worried.

"We've lost a lot of power," he spoke softly so as not to wake Milky. "And we can't hoist the photon sail. I'm afraid we're going to have to dock at the Space Station. They might have a source of power we can adapt." He didn't sound too hopeful and I figured he wasn't too keen to let anyone know we were up here.

But we had no choice. No power, no getting home. And if we didn't get home... Well, that didn't bear thinking about. Drifting off into the emptiness of space wasn't how I wanted to spend the rest of my summer holidays.

# XIII
## Sudden Danger

Somehow, don't ask me how, Caracatus and the Professor managed to get us within range of the Space Station. Imagine a thick ballpoint pen with eight blades stuck out the side - a bit like my dad's Meccano set, the one he never lets me play with. Didn't exactly inspire confidence.

We radioed ahead for permission to dock. Back came a babble of voices and a language we didn't understand. Now this wasn't unusual since the Space Station usually had an international crew. But it should have been a warning. Then a voice, in English, gave us landing instructions so we proceeded.

An arm unwound from one of the sides, ready to attach itself. They were expecting us. With a brief shudder, the Solar Breeze connected and the Professor opened the hatch. Standing in front of us, smiling the most evil smile imaginable, stood Hugh Mungus holding a gun. He gestured us out. We came, stumbling in shock. The Professor didn't even have time to shut down Caracatus which, as it turned out, was a good thing.

Holding Milky and me by the hand, he asked Hugh what was the meaning of this. But the bulky whatever-he-was just kept prodding with his gun and told us to keep moving. The thought did cross my mind - for a split second - that the three of us could take on Hugh Mungus. But then more henchmen appeared, all carrying guns. So scratch that idea.

On entering the main chamber, we saw her: Anna Mustelid. I realised by now, having seen it in Oogli's computer file of animal species, that her name meant 'stoat or weasel'. Suited her. Hands on hips, covered in a dark red spacesuit she looked ready to pounce and tear us limb from limb. "Well," she sneered, "fancy meeting you here." She gave a sinister laugh. Then she walked round us, sizing us up.

"I take it by your stunned expressions that you weren't expecting a welcoming committee? Sorry our previous hosts aren't here to greet you. They had to take an unexpected space walk."

Hugh translated for the benefit of the guards, who laughed uproariously.

The Professor held on to us and fixed her with a cold stare. "What is it you want, Anna?"

"Oh come now, Septimus. Don't play the absent-minded professor with me. You know I want mustelidium and I know you've got it." The faint trace of a smile snaked around her lips. "By the way, congratulations on reaching Mars. Just as I intended." Then her voice became harder, sharper. "So hand it over. Now!"

"We took nothing from Mars," said the Professor calmly. I was impressed that he could be. At a time like this.

A vicious slap hit him so forcefully that he lost his balance - and lost us. Two huge bullies shot forward. One took hold of Milky who scratched him and mine got such a kick on the shins that he fell to the floor. That would make it even then.

Hugh M. jerked the Professor up and pinned him against a console. I thought I was imagining it but it looked like Uncle Septimus was slipping something small and metallic underneath one of the levers. No one else noticed.

Anna came forward and gently led him to a chair. She was trying a new tactic. The Professor motioned to us to come to him. We went. Surprisingly the guards didn't protest. I expect they could see we were at a slight disadvantage. Given that they were tying us up.

"Now, Septimus," Anna was purring, like a cat contemplating dinner - or even Humphrey on the lookout for mice. "Let's be reasonable. My organisation wants you to work for us. You will be well compensated and allowed to research any area you wish. For us. Just give me the samples and we can all go home."

"Even if I had any samples - which I don't - I wouldn't give them to you. You've become deranged, Anna. You've lost any sense of moral responsibility. If you let us go now, I'll make sure you're not prosecuted." He put his arms around us.

Even I could tell that we weren't holding any trump cards here. Anna positively shrieked with laughter. "You seem to forget, Septimus, that I always get what I want. And you and these children are certainly not going to stand in my way." She lunged forward and tore Milky from his hand. "For a start, I'll take back this one. Come to Aunt Anna, precious," she was saying to the crying girl in a voice that could crack glass. "You can keep the other brat," and she threw me one of her ultra-special nasty looks.

"What do you want with the child?"

"She needs to go back to her mummy and daddy so they," and she leered at Uncle Septimus, "will be more cooperative." She strolled over to pinch his cheek. "You see, my dear, we have other scientists working for us. The trouble is they have the same moral scruples as you and need a bit of extra persuasion to make them see sense. My darling sister didn't do the trick so now we need her offspring to increase the pressure," and Anna pushed her face into Milky's so that she let out a scream which nearly deafened us. Good weapon, I thought. It certainly made Anna back off.

I was keeping amazingly cool through all this. Yes, I was scared, who wouldn't be? But danger makes me see things clearly and if ever a situation called for clear vision - or even a plan - this was it. While the Professor was being searched, and trying to assure Anna that he didn't have the mineral she wanted, my mind was whirring. Caracatus must be picking this up. He'd be concerned - inasmuch as a computer can be - about the predicament we were in. Perhaps he could contact the authorities back on Earth - who must have realised their Space Station was being hijacked. But how could they get a spaceship up here in time? Before we were sent out on a spacewalk without life preservers?

I rubbed my wrist to ease the pain of the ropes. Then I felt the watch - and the computer. I switched it on and turned the screen so that it would pick up the image of the Professor tied up. I tapped out S-O-S repeatedly until I caught one of the guards looking at me suspiciously. I smiled at him which made him even more suspicious. He came over. Just at that moment, Milky let rip with another of her famous screams. He clasped his hands over his ears and ran from the chamber.

Phew! That was close. But Milky had seen what I was trying to do and winked at me. Her aunt squealed at her to stop screaming and Milky hung her head in mock shame. Good actress. Great screamer.

The Professor and Anna were still arguing. It almost sounded like he was trying to win time. Which is what I needed to do, too. I was hoping that my message would get through to our friends. What they could do to help us, I didn't know. But I didn't like the thought that these punks were going to get away with it. At least if they were going to kill us, I wanted someone to know about it.

"Hey, Hughey!" I shouted over to the big guy. "How's that fat head of yours? Have you recovered yet from the knock I gave you? Fatso?" Now I admit this sounded suicidal and not something I would ever have tried back home with Murky. But here in space anything seemed possible.

It had the desired effect. The lumbering guard moved away from the Professor and menacingly towards me, smiling as if he were expecting a big treat. I looked over at Milky and winked. She nodded and gave of her best. The scream that echoed round the chamber was several decibels above what could be considered comfortable. Or safe. One after another pane, screen, diode shattered into tiny fragments. We crouched to protect ourselves from flying glass while the guards either fled or started screeching themselves. None so loud as Anna, trying to round them up again.

And then we lifted off, right inside the chamber. It was the strangest thing - we were all completely weightless! Now you'd think I would have gotten used to that by now but I was stunned by this side-effect of Milky's scream. Or so I thought. The Professor recovered first and swam towards us in mid-air to undo our cords. He was directing us towards the entrance where we'd left the Solar Breeze. There was something in his hand - the metallic-looking object I'd seen him hiding. He waved it at the door and with a sudden jerk, it opened!

# XIV
## Rescued Just in Time

Outside were some friendly, bulging eyes looking in. "Max! Professor Boggle! Milky!" Oog was calling and hurrying us along. Already there were guards on our tail, clutching at us. With just a millisecond to spare we leapt the divide that separated the Space Station from the Martian spaceship. Hugh Mungus had lunged after Milky, catching hold of her shirt and pulling it. But the Professor held her firm, pushed me towards Oog and with his free hand, jerked round to plant a whopper right on Hugh Mungus's bullet head. Milky was catapulted towards Moog's waiting arms and the Professor leapt into the ship.

In another nanosecond the spaceship had left the Station far behind. It took us a lot longer to catch our breaths. And then we needed explanations. The Professor first. He returned the metallic object to Oog. "Thank you, my friend. Without this anti-gravity device, we would never have escaped." He saw my questioning look. "Yes, I, too, was given a present I couldn't refuse. And it does contain the mineral Anna wanted. But not in its purest form so I wasn't really lying when I said I didn't have a sample."

I sat down, took the energy drink Oogli gave me, and had the Professor start again. "Our friends have refined what Anna insists on referring to as mustelidium and turned it into a small metal object that can cancel out gravity. Anna had had a similar idea. She was trying to persuade - force - Milky's father to work on it: an anti-gravity device. It could get a spaceship into orbit in no time. Mars in five hours!" He shuddered. "Her organisation controlling space. And heaven knows what other devious purposes she had in mind." He gave me a hug. "But good thinking, Max. If you hadn't contacted our friends, we wouldn't have had quite such a lucky escape."

"Zoog was monitoring your progress after we registered the solar flare," Oog continued. "Our computers were in touch with Caracatus and he informed us of the situation. Once Max showed us the scene inside the Space Station, we knew you needed our help immediately."

"And boy, are we grateful!" I said hugging Oogli, who deserved a lot of the credit.

We toured the Martian spacecraft. You've never seen anything like this! No movie could have prepared me for it. I had just caught a glimpse as I was hauled in: a long silver tube revolving and hovering at the same time. Inside it looked like one of their living pods with mini-biospheres dotted about.

"We like to feel at home on board," said Moog, and it was very homey. "We even have your favourite food, Max - red slugs in green algae." She looked so pleased and I learnt a valuable lesson: never over-praise the cooking.

They'd managed to rescue Caracatus, too, and I passed him in the control module chattering away to the other computers. I suspect he was exaggerating the dangers a bit and his role in our escape but he was entitled. After all there were more computers here than he would ever see in his usable lifespan so he was making the most of it.

I was wondering how they powered this ship. "Proton power," said Zoog.

"How did you know what I was thinking?"

"I keyed into your brainwaves. I hope you don't mind. You were transmitting confusion so I thought I would answer your question." Oh yeah, I forgot you could do that. I also wanted to think, "Stop it, it's getting annoying", but I caught myself in time.

"You see, Max, protons exert an electrical force of repulsion. That means that we are pushed backwards."

I continued to transmit confusion. Oog nodded, "Yes, it is true. Because gravity is so weak up here, the mass increases. We have a lot of mass wanting to create a force but, as you know…"

"Force equals mass times acceleration," Oogli piped up.

"So, we need acceleration," continued Oog, looking proudly at his offspring. "A lot of acceleration."

"And," said Moog, "these protons can provide enormous amounts of acceleration because they are light particles." Now everyone was getting in on the act so I had a go, too.

"And they move at the speed of light?"

"That is right, but as Zoog said, repulsion means we are pushed backwards so we just have to figure out where we are going and let ourselves be pushed backwards." Which, when you think of it, is how a lot of us go through life.

"But it all comes down to acceleration," said Oogli, still adding his share, "which we need in order to leave our planet's gravity. Once we are in space, where there is no gravity, we just keep going until we need to stop."

"Actually stopping is the hardest part," commented Zoog. "I have been working on that."

"Oh, don't I know it," said the Professor. And that got me worrying about going on until the ends of the Universe which, of course, might not have any end. In which case what happened then? Best not to think about it. Which was a good idea because at that moment one of the Martians rushed over with a message for Oog.

He looked round our little circle and his bulging eyes were protruding even more. "It looks like your former friend is pursuing us."

"What! How is that possible?" asked the Professor.

"Our computers show a spacecraft and the fuel is not one with which we are familiar."

"Nuclear-powered?" suggested the Professor.

"Yes, it is possible. We have no supplies of uranium so it is not an option for us. Highly dangerous, I would think. Still, I am impressed by this female's tenacity."

"And I am very angry with this female," snapped Moog, holding onto Milky who had obviously filled her in on Aunt Anna's shortcomings.

"Could they catch us?" I wanted to get back to basics.

Oog shook his head. "No, but our computers show that they have missiles onboard and they could do some damage." Just then, as if to prove the point, there was a thud, a shudder and we were sent sprawling on the floor.

"Now I am mega-angry!" shouted Moog, picking herself up and checking that Milky and I were all right. Oog was shaking both his tentacles at the enemy's spaceship. "I would like to crush them in my metal-basher!" I was going to second that.

The Professor was suggesting something to Oog and he conferred with Zoog and Moog in their language. Oogli raised an objection but was told clearly, so I gathered, that this was one time when he should be seen and not heard. Know how that feels. He stomped off in a sulk and I followed.

"What's going on, Oogli?" I struggled to keep up.

"Oh, the senior Martians want to eliminate the evil female with asteroids." I didn't really have a problem with that. "But it would mean flying through the Asteroid Belt which could be dangerous for us." Now that I did have a problem with.

"So, what's your idea?"

"Dump her into a black hole," and I saw his eyes lighting up.

"Whoa, isn't that even more dangerous? Besides impossible?"

"Not really. As long as we do not pass the accretion disc. If we do that, then we get crushed. Or turn into, what do you call it? Oh yes, spaghetti."

I considered this. Seriously. "So, let's go back to the asteroid plan. How exactly would it work?"

He shrugged. "We plot a trajectory through the asteroids, hoping that her spacecraft cannot keep up and that it gets hit." He laughed derisively. "It is like playing star lottery. Just when you have finished counting them all, another million pop up."

"So why are you keen on the black hole?"

But now he was looking mysterious, as only a Martian can. All he would say was, "It will help me with my experiment." I wasn't reassured.

Milky came to find us. "Come quickly. Moog wants to strap us in. It's going to be a bumpy ride."

We raced back to the control module and Moog put us into flexible harnesses which would allow us to ride out the shock waves. I could already feel the spaceship vibrating. On my computer screen rocks were streaking past. You should have seen the size of these babies! Huge, jagged, lumpy - designed to do maximum damage. I was watching Zoog and Oog steer the ship around hundreds of gigantic boulders. The Professor had a ringside seat and was obviously enjoying the ride. Even I was experiencing a surge of excitement at every asteroid we dodged. One by one, weaving over and under - it was better than Astroball! Of course, the whole point was to lure Anna into the Belt and hopefully zonk her.

I was getting a good view of her spacecraft. It looked just like the Solar Breeze but with nuclear-powered rockets. Whoever was flying her ship knew what they were doing. They kept on our path, diving in and out amongst the rubble, not getting hit at all. I could tell the Martians were impressed. I thought about our Solar Breeze and felt sad that we couldn't have saved our ship.

But being on a Martian Intergalactic Explorer was way better and I was willing to put up with that.

Then the Martians tried a new tack. "Professor, we must catch the next asteroid! It contains the mineral you are looking for." Both their eyes were winking and they pointed to their laser transmitters. They were making sure that Anna would pick up their conversation. The Professor nodded. The ship made a sudden downward movement and right in front - heading straight for us - was the most enormous rock I'd ever seen! Banking sharply to the right, we sailed past with millimetres to spare.

I looked back expecting a huge fireball and fragments of Solar Breeze II. Another second of suspense - and there they were again! An arm from the side of their ship was just being retracted.

They'd managed to reach out and slice a section off the asteroid. But were still after us! Maybe Anna thought a proton-powered spaceship - complete with Martians - would be an even bigger prize.

"Nice try, Septimus! And friends!" the sarcastic voice of Anna Mustelid came over the transmitter. Gosh, this woman was good. Evil, but good - if that was possible. We'd sustained some damage to our protective shield and one of the computers was down. So villains one, aliens zero.

In another minute we'd left the orbit of debris with plan A a failure. But I'd underestimated our Martian friends. Plan B went into action. "Professor, we need your help with this. We are setting a course for the black hole at the centre of our galaxy and…"

"Wait a minute!" I interrupted. "Do you mean 'our' galaxy? This galaxy?"

"Yes. Did you not know there was one?"

"In my nightmares!"

"Relax, Max," said the Professor, the picture of calm. "Our friends know what they're doing." The others nodded, eagerly. Behind him, Oogli was jumping up and down in wild excitement. Great! I was surrounded by mad Martians and about to be turned into spaghetti. I paced back and forth, trying to keep calm. On the overhead screen numbers were flashing past: the mega-warp drive had been activated. I didn't feel a thing. But I had a strange feeling I was about to.

"Where - where is it?" I stammered.

Moog put a comforting tentacle on my shoulder. "Look outside, dear." Through the porthole I could see a disc of light spinning rapidly around a dark centre. Occasionally a brilliant flash ripped through the middle.

"Isn't this amazing, Max?" I'd forgotten about Milky. She did get amazed by the strangest things.

"But this is the thing," I hissed at her, "that swallows everything in its path - everything - and crushes it!"

"Including light," she added. "It disappears forever." Thank you, Milky.

"It also changes the shape and chemical composition of whatever it swallows." Oogli had joined us. Why did he have to keep showing off? Especially with facts that weren't really comforting.

"Do not frighten Max," scolded Moog. Who me? Frightened? "We are only going near the edge, dear. We will be able to recharge our electrical systems and reinforce our protective shield."

"Oh-oh." Zoog's worried voice made everyone jump. Now I was frightened.

"What is wrong?" Oog asked.

"This black hole is very massive. It has a strong magnetic field. Our computers cannot control it. I think we will fly around the other side."

"What about Anna?" I checked. She was still out there.

"The plan is that she follows us and becomes sucked into the hole."

Simple, neat. I liked it.

Suddenly something flashed onto the screen. The others crowded round and I couldn't see what it was. Moog decided we needed "sustenance" and marched us off. I wasn't feeling too much like eating - unusually - but she hurried us into another chamber. Before we had a chance to tuck into a Martian energy meal, the Professor arrived, saying Moog was needed back in the control room.

He sat down and tried to smile reassuringly but I recognised the bushy sideburns.

"You're worried, aren't you, Professor?"

"To tell you the truth, Max, I am. I'm sure our Martian friends know what they're doing but this is a super massive black hole - three million times the mass of the Sun." He paused and frowned. "It's one of the most destructive forces in the universe. Nothing can escape its pull. Space is changed. Gas and stars fall into it, never to be seen again." Okay, enough of the lecture; what's the bottom line here? "But," he smiled, "there's really nothing to worry about." Well, five out of ten for trying.

Oogli had been following the proceedings in the command module on his laser transmitter. "Oh yes, there is. I have just heard Zoog say that we have overshot the accretion disc."

The Professor went a whiter shade of pale. Milky and I competed for green. "Do you mean…?"

Oogli nodded, not looking well himself. "Yes. We are falling into the black hole!"

# XV
## The Black Hole

Okay, so here was the scene. We were on a Martian spaceship, a damaged Martian spaceship, being pursued by a mad scientist and her evil henchmen. And to top it all off, we were falling into a black hole. Should I be worried? Oh, yes.

But the Professor was smoothing down his sideburns and transmitting through to the command module. "Have we passed the outer event horizon?"

"Negative."

"Then there's still time. Come with me, Max, Oogli, Milky."

"What?" I was trying to ask but the Professor was talking to himself again. I avoided looking at Milky because I didn't want to see her lower lip tremble. Oogli, however, was beaming all the colours of the rainbow. "I think I understand. We have not yet reached the inner event horizon."

"Is that good?" From where I was standing, looking out at a cloud of whirling gas which was threatening to suck us in and crush us into a shapeless mass, inner/outer didn't make a lot of difference.

When we reached the others, the Professor was speaking excitedly to Oog and Zoog. "But don't you see?

If we can tilt the spaceship to go in at an angle, we'll go through the ring. If we stay like this, we'll be crushed!"

"But we do not know what is on the other side of a black hole," said Oog, trying to sound calm. "Nobody does."

"It's got to be better than getting crushed!" Oogli and I shouted out at the same time. Beat that.

"And our directional computer is non-operational," continued Zoog.

"I've modelled just this sort of scenario on Caracatus," said the Professor who never ceased to amaze me. "I know it can be done." Oog and Zoog looked at each other, unconvinced. Moog thought it sounded pretty risky, Oogli and I were all for it. Milky was still snivelling. But it was the only plan we had.

Caracatus was snoozing when we started him up and rather grumpy. "This is really important, Caracatus," explained the Professor. "We need you to drive this spaceship through a black hole. Just as we rehearsed."

With a whirr and a couple of short bangs, our computer sprang to life. "Oh, is that all? Right. What do you want me to do?" Suddenly there was a slightly louder bang. "What did you say? A black hole?" Caracatus' voice had lost some of its confidence.

"Oh please, Caracatus," Milky put her arm around him. "If you don't help us, we'll be crushed to spaghetti."

Just like a girl, I thought, always the drama queen. But I had to admit she produced a convincing argument.

It did the trick, With lights pulsing and electronic impulses surging, he allowed himself to be programmed. The Martians lent assistance with their remaining computers but I could tell Caracatus was enjoying being top dog.

"This is quite a massive black hole," the computer was saying.

"How massive?" asked the Professor.

"Ten million solar masses." Pretty massive then.

"We need to overcome gravity by spinning," said the Professor. "That will act as a counterbalance to the force from the hole. If we can tilt at the right angle, we can slide through."

Zoog was still shaking his head. "Nothing has ever gone through a black hole. It is just not possible."

"It's not impossible either!" I said, with every confidence in the Professor. Well, quite a lot of confidence.

Oog agreed. "We have got to try. It is our only chance. Now everyone into their body straps."

Outside the windows it was getting darker and darker. Our spaceship was beginning to spin faster and faster. There wasn't a moment to lose!

"Caracatus, have you programmed our angle of descent?" The Professor was sounding as close to calm as he could get.

"Affirmative. We are entering the black hole at 33.3 degrees. We will escape the vortex."

"Hopefully," I heard Zoog say under his breath.

"Hold on tight!" shouted the Professor as the spaceship began to push forward. We gripped with all our strength, but even so we were being tipped this way and that, pirouetting round one another. I was beginning to feel seasick and Milky didn't look too good either. I hoped that if she was going to throw up, she'd be tilted away from me.

"It is good that this is a super-massive black hole," whispered Oogli to me. And that would be good how? "It means we have a shallower slope to fall down. We will not be stretched so much." Oh yeah, I was beginning to feel much better already. "And if we miss the singularity, we will be all right."

"What's singularity?" I asked weakly.

"Well, that would crush you. It is a very strong force." Somehow Oogli sensed I wasn't too happy to hear this.

"Do not worry, Max," said Moog, "we are still spinning. And that is good."

"But we've got to be careful to avoid the centre," said the Professor, concentrating on the instruments.

"Well, we are approaching from the poles, so there is every chance that we will come out the other end," Oog was sounding much more positive now.

"If the tunnel does not collapse," added Zoog, gloomily.

"What's at the other end?" I asked, almost wishing I hadn't.

"Perhaps another Universe," said the Professor. "If we can find one."

"Or a white hole." Don't ask me why I said it, I guess I was trying to be funny or something. After all everyone else was coming up with weird statements, one more wasn't going to attract any attention.

But everyone was staring at me, then at each other. "Of course!" said Oog, sounding really excited. "We could use its energy to eject out the other end!"

"Yes," said the Professor, looking thoughtful, "a white hole is the opposite of a black hole. So..." he looked over at me, smiling. "Well done, Max."

"If the white hole can generate anti-gravity," said Zoog, quickly typing in formulae and coordinates, "we might be able to..."

"Create a wormhole!" cried the Professor, jumping up and hitting his head on the ceiling. I thought he'd flipped what with all these holes but he was beaming at me like I was brilliant or something.

"Correct!" continued Zoog. "We are in the right force field. Because this star was so massive, there will be two mouths to the tunnel. We can leave by the second one."

"How about the tunnel?" asked the Professor. "Is it stable?"

"Stable," confirmed Moog, checking her calculations. "At the moment. But I cannot guarantee that it will not collapse."

"We can push the walls of the wormhole apart with anti-matter," said Oog, helping Zoog at the control panel. "We still have some stored in our reserve tank." He looked over at me. "Well done, Max." I shrugged modestly, it was nothing really.

But my mind was whirring. I'd picked up a thing or two from working with the Professor. "Wait a minute. Wouldn't it be better to use the anti-matter to cancel out the gravity from the black hole. That way we could go back the way we came in. Couldn't we, Professor?" I thought I'd better check.

The Professor was nodding, slowly and reluctantly. I figured he was disappointed at not getting to see another universe. "Yes, Max. That would be best." He looked at Oog and Zoog. "Otherwise, we don't know what we'll find." They were agreeing now. "Well done, Max." Three in one day, this felt good.

Not for long though. Oogli hadn't been joining in. He was sulking again. "Hey, Oogli, aren't you pleased? We're going to get out of this thing."

He turned away from me. "You have ruined my experiment," he said. He still wouldn't tell me what it was.

# XVI
## Max Saves the Day

Just then, with everything going so well, who should come back into our solar system? Of course, Anna Mustelid, the evil one. We'd forgotten all about her, obviously having had other things on our mind.

Another "Oh," from Zoog alerted us. "We cannot return the way we came in," he said. "There is an object blocking the entrance. It is generating an even more powerful force." We all crowded round the screens. One by one they went dead. Whatever this new energy was, it was capable of cancelling out the anti-gravity that we were generating. The Professor was communicating with Caracatus again, asking him to identify the source.

Turned out to be her spacecraft, nuclear-powered, feeding off the edge of the black hole. The more neutrons the accretion disc was emitting, the more energy her ship was able to absorb and generate. And that was not good news for us.

"We cannot switch off the black hole," Oog was saying. "They are feeding from it and keeping the power supply open."

"And if we do try to go out that way, we'll run straight into them," the Professor added. Ironic, wasn't it? It was supposed to be Anna in this hole, not us.

Suddenly, another computer went down. "She is sucking too much power from us," said Zoog. "If we do not get out of here soon …" Nobody dared finish his sentence.

"What about Max's first plan? The white hole? Then we could get out by the other tunnel." So Milky had been paying attention.

"Yes, our only way. Caracatus, change of plan." Given that we'd messed him around a bit and there was every likelihood of his being condensed into molecules, too, Caracatus was taking it pretty well.

While the others were occupied with last minute calculations and programming Caracatus, Oogli whispered to me to follow him. We released our body straps and floated off down one of the tunnels to a cube which had been strictly off-limits. The little Martian pushed some numbers on the panel at the side. "I have the combination," he said in answer to my surprised look. "Come in, quick."

"What is this? What goes on here?" I was a little worried about the hissing and harrumphing. Even Caracatus on a bad day didn't sound like this. Next to a vat of flashing light, sat one of the space saucers from the Astroball tournament.

"It is my experiment," said Oogli, "but I will explain that later." He looked at me quizzically. "How much do you know about time travel?"

"Time travel? What? Nothing!" And that's how I wanted to keep it.

"Oh dear," continued Oogli, "then I will have to start at the beginning."

"I wish you would." Although I didn't. All I wanted was to get out of the hole we were in and swap places with Anna.

"Well, you know that wormholes are shortcuts to very distant places in curved space?"

"No, but do go on."

"Well, they are. And we're about to create one with the anti-gravity from the white hole. And that," and he was positively vibrating with excitement, "will take us very fast to the other side of the Universe. Or to other universes."

"Whoa! Why do we want to go there?"

Oogli looked at me with surprise. "But you want to find out what is out there? Are you not the slightest bit curious about our Universe?"

"I am!" said a small voice behind us.

I spun round so fast I did a somersault in mid-air. "What are you doing here?" I asked an angelic-looking Milky.

"I snuck in behind you. You didn't even notice!" she laughed.

"Well, you can sneak right back out again," I said, getting really annoyed. If we were going exploring, the last thing we needed was some scatty girl. Even though she was a good screamer and knew a thing or two about science. Which might come in handy in another universe. Wait a minute, what was I thinking?

"And how does this help us to get out of here?"

"Well," Oogli carried on, "if we go at the speed of light, we can go forward in time. But if we find a wormhole - which we will now - we can go backwards."

I could see I had to humour him. "Okay, sorry not to get more excited about this, but I really don't think we should be messing with time." I put a hand on one of Oogli's tentacles. "Let's leave exploring other universes for next time and think of Plan B."

He looked disappointed. Obviously humans were beyond him. "Very well. Let me show you what we can do." He was vibrating again. "These are the reserve tanks of anti-gravity. I have managed to harness it to my space-saucer. We could sneak back out the way we came in. The saucer is smaller than our ship and will not be picked up by their radar. Then once our spaceship is out the other end, we can push the enemy into the black hole."

I could see a whole mess of trouble we would be getting into. What was it with these holes that was turning everyone's brains to mush? "How do you think this weeny saucer is going to push a big nuclear-powered spaceship? Have you gone crazy?"

He looked puzzled. "I do not know what crazy is but I can generate enough anti-gravity to get us out. And once we are at the mouth of the hole, I will focus the anti-matter onto the accretion disc which will create a force field - like an enormous sucking mouth!"

"How exciting!" Milky was clapping her hands. "Let's do it!"

"Am I the only voice of reason here?" I said in desperation. "We're small," and I pinched finger and thumb together, "and they're huge!" and I held my arms far apart. "This just isn't possible."

"Max," Milky put her hand on my arm and looked at me sweetly, "it's not impossible either."

"Okay let me think." What would the Professor do? "How fast would we be travelling?"

"Close to the speed of light."

"Right. So, at the moment our spaceship is suspended in the inner event horizon, hoping to harness the white hole at the other end. But you can get us back outside, hoping nobody notices?"

Some hope.

Oogli nodded. "Yes, that is correct."

"Now, we still have the problem of Anna. But if we can keep her from firing her missiles at us and make sure we don't fall in again, we might just be able to - I can't believe I'm saying this - nudge her spaceship in?" They were both smiling.

My mind was whirring again. "No, too risky. Any chance of Plan C?"

Just then it went dark, pitch black accompanied by a violent rocking. I could hear the Professor's voice over the transmitter, calling to us. I tried to call back but there was no answer. Okay, no time to think. This called for action.

We groped our way into Oogli's saucer. Luckily the system was self-contained and had emergency lights. We fired up the engines and eased out of the spaceship's docking port. I was still trying to reach the others to assure them we were safe. Finally I got through to Caracatus. "What's going on?"

"We have sustained a direct hit from enemy spacecraft. All safe. Damage to power systems. Please give location."

"Tell the Professor we're okay. Keep the spacecraft tilted at 33.3 degrees. When I transmit a signal, fire up your remaining engines and go. We'll meet you at the other end." I thought it best not to tell them exactly where we were in case they didn't understand. Or approve. We didn't have time to argue.

Oogli was as good as his word. His engines were operating at full speed and ahead of us we could see the whirling light of the accretion disc. We could also see the hovering shape of Solar Breeze II and sparks flashing into and out of the black hole. But there was something else which looked even more unnerving. A huge concave mirror was suspended in front of the spacecraft causing the brightness which was almost blinding us.

Even Oogli looked panicked. He said he'd never seen anything like it but that they must be sending lasers into the black hole.

"And back again with that mirror," I said, trying to work out what this could mean. I wasn't going to get nervous just yet and the warning look I gave Milky told her, "Whatever you do, do not scream!"

We were manoeuvring past the beams, staying close to the edge. I shut down the communication system so there was no chance they would pick up our signal. But I was holding my breath. With a final burst of speed we managed to ease out underneath the ship. Their reflective mirror succeeded in masking the blip that would have been our tiny craft. Luckily.

But then I had a scary thought which I ran past Oogli. "The light bouncing back gains energy, right?" Oogli nodded; he was following me. "And it's not dispersing, their spacecraft is acting as a plug. Which must mean?" I was going to let him finish, just in case I was wrong. Which I was hoping I was.

Oogli nodded, "Yes, pressure is building up. The Hole will explode."

"Oh!" cried Milky, "They'll be blown to bits! Moog!"

"That is not all," said Oogli. "When the hole explodes, it releases uranium. They will contaminate our whole Solar System."

"No, they won't!" I was shouting now. This woman had turned my friend into a zombie, kidnapped her parents, held us hostage and was about to blow up my great-uncle and our Martian friends. Not to mention all that pollution! She was one grade A bully. And I was tired of being bullied.

My mind was working overtime. "Get our ship on the transmitter, Milky, and tell them to programme Caracatus to re-start all the engines as soon as the power comes back on. I'm going to help Oogli. They're going to get one almighty push."

Just then Oogli's eyes bulged - sign of maximum panic. "Look out there, Max!" I looked - just in time to see a missile whizzing past us. It twirled our saucer round like a spinning top, pushing us against our seats - knocking Oogli out. Oh-oh, this was getting serious.

"Max!" Milky was bordering on a scream. "You've got to take over! You've got to save them!"

My reactions kicked in. I grabbed the controls. I'd already proved to myself that I was a fast learner and if Oogli's calculations were correct, we could generate just enough anti-matter to block up Anna's engines. Then - with a flick, like playing Astroball - we could tip them into the black hole. The force of them falling in would create enough pressure to push our ship out. That was the theory.

But then I had another idea - "just like Astroball". Of course!

"Milky, keep a lookout for missiles. Shout out when you see the next one."

I waited for Milky's "Now!" and headed off. Dodging, diving, I kept up with the projectile, just a bit bigger than the asteroid I'd been so good at dribbling. I wove the space saucer underneath, bouncing the missile from side to side, deflecting it, curving it back. Maneuvering it round the back of the enemy spacecraft. I was imagining Anna and Hugh Mungus looking out their porthole, going: "ARRGGGHHH!!!"

Then with one final flip, angling it just the way I'd done for that final goal, I lobbed the missile straight at them. The explosion, so near the edge, was brighter than a galaxy forming. A split second later, all the debris was sucked in as if the black hole had been waiting for a more substantial meal. It looked like a giant swirly! Murky would have been impressed.

"Oh, Max! You've done it! You've really done it!" There was an embarrassing note of hero-worship in Milky's voice. No time for that now. We had to make contact and get back to our spaceship and hope that Oogli was all right. That everyone was all right.

I wish I'd had more time to take in the view. Ahead was a void in space, belching out particles of light and dust. Surrounding us were bright stars, a lone comet, in the distance planets. And further out? Who knows? We'd missed our chance to explore other universes, but we'd saved this one. Not bad for a night's work.

Suddenly Oog's voice came over loud and clear, "Where are you? Please report position." I transmitted back, filled in the bare facts. I could hear the Professor whooping in the background.

Milky was pointing out of the porthole. Just ahead was the Martian Explorer. My theory had worked: they'd been blown out the other end by the force of Anna's ship being sucked in. Because they'd maintained their angle of descent, they'd escaped the ring of singularity. And hadn't been turned into spaghetti.

By now Oogli had come to. Milky was shaking him and telling him about the amazing things I'd done, which I was having a hard time believing myself. I had to run through it all again once we'd entered the ship, although Milky was doing most of the talking. I was trying hard not to blush, they were making such a fuss of me. Everyone was so happy - and relieved - to see one another and what with all the explanations and the excitement, I just fell asleep where I stood.

"I'm not really a hero," I remember saying, as the Professor put me to bed. I saw him smile and heard, "Maybe a hero is someone who doesn't know it yet."

# XVII
## Re-entry

When I woke up, Earth orbit was approaching. It was better that way: no time for lengthy goodbyes. The Martians were going to drop us off but were doing their best to persuade us to visit again. We knew that we needed to get back to our families and our world but promised we'd see them sometime. They gave us computer watches, so we could stay in touch. Caracatus was allowed to go back with them. We owed him that much.

The sky was turning a hazy pink as we landed. Just our luck, old Joe was out walking his dog and he ran screaming down the road, calling out, "The Martians have landed! The Martians have landed!" Luckily, given the sort of town it was, nobody was going to pay much attention.

We did a group hug, wiped away a bit of moisture and waved until the ship was out of sight, just a vapour trail in the stratosphere. I didn't want to go home just yet so I stayed outside the Professor's house while he made some calls. I kept looking up in the sky, searching for I didn't know what. Just trying to take it all in.

Humphrey sauntered past and asked how my trip had been. I told him, he laughed, said he didn't believe it. But that he was glad that Caracatus wouldn't be coming back, maybe now there'd be some peace around here. Maybe.

The Professor came back outside with Milky. Turned out his contacts in the government had freed her mum and dad and they were waiting at the airport to take her home. She held out a tear-stained hand, said she'd never forget me. I couldn't help myself - I kissed her. Told her to come back sometime.

They dropped me off. The Professor said to take care, he'd see me soon. He had a funny look when he waved goodbye, then called me back and said, "Just remember, Max, reality will still be here when you're least aware of it."

I nodded. I'd have to remember that.

# XVIII
## Back Home

The reception at home was pretty welcoming. My mum hugged me and told me how much she'd missed me. She'd even baked my favourite cake but I'd sort of gone off cake. My dad surprised me by hugging me, too, and saying how well I looked. And how much he'd missed me!

We sat down and had a nice family meal, no phone going, no interruptions, just my parents and I talking. Of course, I had to change my story a bit: Astroball became basketball and exploring outer space became orienteering. I turned Anna into this mean counsellor whom they got rid of. I left out the bit about the black hole.

My dad announced that he was getting a job closer to home. He looked at me sort of funny and said he was sorry for all the times he hadn't been there and that was going to change now. And if I wanted any help with my homework, he'd make the time. And we'd be taking that trip to the mountains next holiday. My mum said she was cutting back on her clients, so that she'd be home when I got back from school. You could have knocked me over with Martian dust!

But the best welcome-home surprise came a few days later when I had to go back to school. Yes, I know I was never a fan of school but this time was different. Maybe because of all the adventures I'd had and the friends I'd made, or the long talks I was having with my parents - I felt good about myself. And I looked it!

On arriving in class, I could see people staring at me. Where it had bothered me before, this time there was curiosity, interest and even a "Hi, Max!" or two. Murky was still loitering in the corner, glaring at me. But even he looked surprised. I'd slimmed down a lot on Martian food and all that exercise had really built up my muscles. Maybe he was thinking twice about taking me on.

Come lunchtime I was feeling like this could be a much better year. I'd talked to some of the people from my last class who seemed much friendlier. And I met this really nice girl, Amelia, who'd just moved into town. We went to the cafeteria together, with a few of my friends.

But there was still this nagging fear in the pit of my stomach. Out of the corner of my eye I could see Murky pinning a smaller boy to the wall and taking his lunch money. Then he sauntered over to our table with two of his gang. He went past me and my stomach unknotted. Suddenly he lunged forward and grabbed Amelia's lunchbox - she was so startled she didn't know what to do!

The other kids avoided her gaze and carried on talking as if nothing unusual had just happened.

Then she looked at me and I saw a tear slowly curving down her cheek.

"That's it!" I got up and looked as threatening as I felt. "I've had enough of this!"

I marched over to his table. "Hey, Murky, you big fat turkey!" A hush fell over the dining hall. It sort of reminded me of that time in the Space Station. "You have something that belongs to my friend."

"Oh yeah? What ya gonna do about it?"

Split-second thought: call the Martians. But no, I could handle this bully on my own.

"You and me. No one else." I put out an arm to deflect his henchmen. They both backed off. There must have been something in my voice and the way I glared at Murky because he didn't look too confident either.

"I'll arm-wrestle you for the lunchbox. And you've got to give back all the money you've taken today." I thought it wouldn't hurt to play to the crowd.

Murky burst out laughing, "You weeny! You think you can take me? Right, let's see you try."

We sat down at either side of the table. By now a small crowd had formed, luckily no teacher in sight. We locked hands and pushed, every muscle straining. I held firm, but beads of sweat were forming on Murky's face. He was also grunting a bit, which was rather disgusting. I gave him the Martian squeeze until I could see his eyes crossing. Then I thought I'd better put him out of his misery and get back to my lunch. With one swift downward motion I pinned his arm to the table. He couldn't believe it! Neither could anyone else.

"Two out of three!" he cried out. I agreed and pinned him down again. And again, taking even less time. I was beginning to get bored. A cheer went up from the crowd as more kids ran up to see what had happened.

I thought I might finish off with a swirly but didn't see the point. My triumph was complete. I gave Amelia back her lunchbox; she gave me a look which said, "My hero!" I left Murky paying back the kids whose money he had stolen: there was quite a queue.

When I got home that afternoon, Mum was waiting for me. Rumour had spread that I'd been fighting. I think Murky's mother had phoned and complained. Typical. I explained what had happened, and to Dad when he came home. He was rather proud of me for standing up for myself - and others. Mum was still worried and made me promise not to. I promised. I didn't think I'd need to teach Murky any more lessons.

And I was right. He left me alone after that. In fact, he avoided me and my friends completely. And all the other kids who'd been bullied by him pointed me out. You could say I became a sort of legend.

My classes were going pretty well, too. Teachers, who last year had seen me as some sort of moron were calling on me more often. Of course, I didn't always know the right answer, but I made a pretty good stab at it. Other kids treated me with more respect and I was elected class president. Even Murky voted for me!

But something was missing. The Professor had shut up his house and gone off travelling with the Martians. I had instructions not to say anything. He said it wouldn't be safe. They're somewhere near Alpha Centauri right now. I get regular updates on my wristwatch computer. Humphrey came to live with us. Still grumpy, although occasionally he talks to me. To no one else.

But you want to know why they locked me up. Well, like most heroes, I slipped up. It was in science class. I was doing pretty well but I just got too cocky. When the science teacher - you know, the boring one - asked us what we knew about Mars, I reeled off a list of facts. Some of which, obviously, Mr Hickey didn't know. He was getting more and more annoyed, saying I was talking rubbish. Which made me angry. And you know what I'm like when I get angry. So when he asked how I knew all this stuff was true, I told him, "I was there this summer."

Well, that did it. Kids started laughing, then backed away - liked the tide going out. Teachers got worried, especially when I kept insisting it was true. Because I hate being called a liar, and an idiot, when I know I'm telling the truth.

My parents were tearing their hair out. I could see they wanted to stand by me but it was just too difficult for them. And they couldn't get in touch with Uncle Septimus to find out what had happened this summer. And I wouldn't have wanted to get him into trouble.

So they agreed to let them take me away. They come to visit but my mum cries a lot. They've allowed me to keep Humphrey. He's started digging a tunnel.

So, was Mars - and outer space - everything I thought it would be? Well, yes and no. It was incredibly vast and beautiful and so amazing. It made me realise how truly precious our Earth is and how we should take better care of it. And I know I was really privileged to experience something no one else has.

I know I'll get back there one day. The Professor will come for me. Or the Martians. And I have a plan... -